I0636246

ECHOES *FROM* ACROSS *THE* STREET

Short Stories On Love, Loss and Everything in Between

 Scribe

Echoes From Across The Street

Publisher: Inkscribe Publishing Pvt. Ltd.

PB ISBN Number: 978-1-966421-77-1

Contents

One

The Other Side of the Door

Prajkta Lad

Shreya felt the latch slip from her fingers for half a second before the door shut with a thud. The sound echoed along the narrow corridor of the fourth floor. She stood in place, back turned towards her flatmate, Mihika, her hand hovering above the door knob. She stared at the lock as if her sheer will could reverse the time. The cold brass lock stared back at her, unbothered by her worry.

"Please tell me you have the keys," Shreya asked her flatmate. Her eyes were still fixed on the closed door.

"Huh?" Mihika looked up from her phone hearing the question. "What? Why—" The remaining words stuck in her throat as Shreya turned around. "You did *not.*"

Shreya shrugged with a sheepish smile pasted on her face. "It was all unintentional."

"My keys are on my desk," Mihika answered, "I thought you picked yours." She added, her cheeks pink beneath the corridor's flickering tube light. It seemed it could die any moment, drowning them in the darkness.

Shreya exhaled. This couldn't be happening. They hadn't made it through the last twelve hours—almost crushed themselves on the Western Line, dodged the ankle-length monsoon puddles, and survived the first-week pitches at the digital education start-up that had lured them from their hometowns—only to be defeated by a door. She pressed her back against the peeling ivory paint of 4B and slid to the floor, the indigo of her kurti pooling around her crossed legs.

Outside, Mumbai roared: auto-rickshaws honked in manic competition, the rain was loud against the windows of the corridor, and vendors chanted the virtues of roasted *bhutta* and *masala chai*. In the corridor, though the noise felt distant, muffled by the storeys of concrete, it was still persistent. A lot like the city itself. It was nothing like Dehradun, the city she had grown up in.

Mihika squatted beside her flatmate. "We could ring the landlord."

"His office closes at six. And remember the whole 'Call me only if the building is on fire' speech." Shreya rubbed her temples. A film of humid sweat rolled down her forehead.

"Fine," Mihika huffed, equally exhausted. "Locksmith?"

Shreya glanced at the rain outside before turning to Mihika. "I don't think we'd find one willing to come in this weather any time soon. We'd be lucky if someone came before midnight."

"So, what are we going to do? Sit in this dying disco light and wallow in self-pity?" Mihika asked. "My phone is almost dead. Would give up before I do." She added glancing at her screen.

Shreya didn't answer and looked back at the window.

Taking the lack of a reply as her cue, Mihika also moved her gaze to the window.

And they sat, two twenty-something strangers-turned-flatmates, who had known each other for exactly three weeks. Long enough to share mobile hotspots but not childhood secrets. Neither spoke, both nursing the same fear: that this vast, glittering city would swallow them whole and no one would ever notice.

"I wish Maa was here. She always knows how to handle a crisis," Mihika said after a few minutes.

Shreya had noticed this about Mihika—how everything about her tied back to her mother. She didn't know much. But from what she had gathered over the past few days, she had understood that what Mihika wanted most in life was to become half the woman her mother was. Growing up with a single mother, who had carried storms on her back, Mihika was raised with the strong belief there was not a single problem in this world her mother couldn't find a solution to.

"But I'm glad my parents are not here," Shreya replied, "I don't need another reminder of how incompetent I am." A hollow chuckle escaped her lips. Mihika looked at her for a moment and Shreya wondered if her flatmate would try to make her feel better. When Mihika didn't say anything, she was grateful. No one in the past two decades had been able to make her feel better. And she didn't want them to try.

Another silence filled the corridor.

After what seemed like an eternity, there was a soft click and the door of flat 4A opened a cautious arm's width. Warm yellow light spilled across the corridor's floor, chasing away the gloomy tube-light glow. A woman's face appeared, pale, curious, framed by dark curls pulled into a loose bun.

"Everything okay?" she asked, her voice low but carrying.

Mihika was quick to rise, brushing the imaginary dust from her trousers. "We…um…locked ourselves out. Third week in the city and life's already a mess." She finished with a nervous laugh.

The woman's lips curved up. "That's rough." She opened the door wider. Dressed in a simple peach-coloured kurti and salwar and barely visible pearl studs, she had *haldi* smudged on her sleeve. It was the kind of domestic badge someone like Shreya could never earn. She was lucky that Mihika was not a disaster in the kitchen. "I'm Anagha. Do you want to wait inside? Don't want my new neighbours to serve dinner to the mosquitoes."

Mihika glanced at Shreya, an unspoken exchange between the two: *can we trust her?* A city of millions taught you caution. But Anagha's demeanour felt safe. Gentle like the first showers after an April heat wave.

"If you're sure, we aren't imposing," Shreya said.

"Positive. I was about to eat. Extra dal is never wasted," Anagha replied with a smile.

●●●

Stepping inside Anagha's house was like crossing worlds. Where their 4B still smelled of fresh paint and unopened moving boxes, her 4A was filled with a lived-in coziness: sandalwood *dhoop* lingered in the curtains, terracotta planters nurtured *tulsi*, a money plant, and roses on the inner sill, and the aroma of spices mingled with the air.

Books dominated one wall: Hindi, Marathi, English, and even a sprinkling of Urdu. Shreya noted how most of them were poetry collections. Above them, fairy lights were looped in lazy waves. Photos filled the gaps: Anagha laughing with an elderly couple in front of Pune's

Shaniwaar Wada, her at Marine Drive holding hands with a tall man whose grin reached his eyes, and her cradling a new-born swaddled in daffodil-yellow.

"Dump your bags anywhere," Anagha said, clearing the folded laundry from the maroon two-seater. "I work from home, so the lines between work and home mostly blur."

Shreya nodded and carefully sat on one side of the couch, while Mihika looked around taking in the interiors with genuine curiosity. "You love reading…" she commented.

"Yes, I work as a translator," Anagha answered, filling two glasses with water from the jug kept on the counter on the half-wall separating the kitchen from the living room.

"You translate full-time?" Mihika asked, taking one glass and settling beside Shreya, who thanked Anagha with a small smile as she took the other one.

Anagha nodded. "Mostly. Hindi novels, Marathi poetry, and occasional legal agreements when rent looms."

Shreya's eyes drifted to the collection of Urdu poems but she kept the question to herself. She didn't know the story of those poems and if Anagha hadn't said anything, it meant it was nothing Shreya should ask about. "You've got a beautiful house." She added instead.

"Thank you." Anagha smiled at her. "Dinner's ready. Do you want to wait or we can sit together?"

Mihika and Shreya exchanged another look. "Let's eat," Mihika said and Shreya nodded in agreement.

They sat around the small coffee table. Stainless steel plates, thick-rimmed glasses, and mismatched spoons. Dinner materialized: fluffy rice, dal tempered with garlic and cumin, fried bhindi dusted with aamchur and coriander, and papad roasted directly over the open flame.

"It's nothing fancy," Anagha said, a bit embarrassed.

"It's home," Mihika replied, her stomach growling in approval. "And that's all that matters."

They ate. Conversations began politely with complaints of the weather and local train hacks but soon deepened in the way talk sometimes did when strangers shared fresh home-cooked meals.

Anagha talked of her childhood in Pune's Sadashiv Peth, of sneaking into cinemas to meet her husband, Kartik, whom she had met at a literary festival where she had helped him understand a few verses of a Marathi poem. She also told them how she moved to Mumbai after marriage, drawn by his job designing residential complexes for the BMC, and how they had worked together to make this place she now called home.

Mihika, who didn't miss the longing in Anagha's voice, asked what had happened.

"A drunk driver near CST," Anagha said, her voice steady but her grip on the glass tightening. "Two years ago…he was coming home from work."

Her words fell like pebbles dropped into a still pond. Soft but rippling out far.

Silence washed over the table. The kind that wasn't comfortable but reverent. Outside the rain continued with earnest taps against the window glass like it was trying to become a part of their conversation.

"I'm sorry," Shreya whispered, almost inaudible.

Anagha inhaled, releasing her grip. "It's…fine. Life happens, right?" she said with a smile that didn't reach her eyes. "Some days I translate love letters and forget the void. Other days I stare at one word…*absence*…wishing it swallows everything around it."

The rain picked up again, harder now, like it was grieving too.

Shreya knew it was not as effortless as Anagha made it sound. Losing the person, you thought you would spend all your life with was not easy. It wasn't easy for Anagha. It hadn't been easy for her.

Shreya looked down at her hands, remembering a different ache, a different goodbye. It struck her how easily grief recognized its mirror in others…how unspoken things hummed like a low note held for too long.

Outside, thunder rolled gently in the distance making Shreya wonder if the storm inside her would ever calm.

●●●

After washing plates, with Anagha waving them off with "Tomorrow your turn", they carried cups of coffee to the balcony, a sliver of space jutting over the lane where auto-rickshaws queued. Rain fell from the torn night sky mingling with the sweet smell of *raat-rani* from the neighbour's balcony.

The three perched on the small stools, knees almost touching. Fairy lights blinked overhead, reflecting in the puddles below like constellations fallen on Earth.

Mihika broke the quiet. "Do you ever feel lonely here?" The question sounded dangerously tender.

Shreya also waited for Anagha's answer.

Anagha's eyes were fixed on the lane below where a dog curled beneath a Maruti to escape the downpour. "Yes…" she started slowly, "but loneliness in Mumbai hits different…it hums. Trains pass, people shout, neighbours fight over parking space. The city reminds you...you're not a ghost. Just waiting for something."

"Why do you still live here? Why not go back to Pune, to your parents?" Shreya blurted. She hadn't intended to say it loud but the question was out before she could think it over. Anagha and Mihika turned to her. "Sorry, I shouldn't have asked."

"It's fine," Anagha assured with a smile. "You're not the first to ask. Anyone who comes to know about Kartik does the same."

"And what do you say?" Mihika added.

"That this city is home now," Anagha answered, "we have so many memories here. Leaving this place behind feels like leaving him behind. And I don't think I want that."

Shreya and Mihika didn't say more but their eyes reflected their understanding. They finished the rest of their coffees in silence, looking at the rain that showed no signs of mercy.

●●●

At 10:31 p.m., power flickered. The fan inside coughed to a halt, fairy lights died, fridge beeped its last. Streetlights went down one by one until the only glow was from their phone screens.

"Load shedding," Anagha sighed. "Welcome to suburban glamour."

Mihika titled her screen upwards, casting eerie shadows on their faces. "Please tell me this won't last long."

"Well, it could have been worse." Anagha shrugged her shoulders which suggested she had seen worse too many times to count. Mihika groaned. Shreya checked her phone. The battery could die any time now. She audibly sighed wondering what more turns were these twenty-four hours going to take.

"We were locked out earlier, and now there's a power out," Mihika said, "what's next? A monsoon flooding through the window?"

As if summoned by her sarcasm, thunder growled in the distance. The three women glanced at each other and burst into laughter. It was the kind of laughter that came without invitation—deep, from the belly. The one that felt warm, kind, and earned.

"Be careful what you wish for Mihika," Shreya commented. Mihika gestured zipping her mouth. Anagha chuckled at her antics.

"Okay," Anagha said, "we are not sleeping through this. Are we?"

"Nope," Mihika agreed. "Let's do something old-school. Truth or dare?"

Shreya raised an eyebrow. "With no way to do any dares?"

"Guess we are trapped with only truths then, much like adulthood," Anagha added.

Mihika grabbed a cushion. "Truth," she declared.

Anagha leaned forward. "What's something you have never told anyone? Not even your mother."

Shreya wondered if there was anything Mihika had not shared with her mother. From what she knew, Mihika was close to her Maa. The kind of close that included daily phone calls and shared recipes through voice notes. *Could any secrets live in that space?*

Mihika thought for a moment, chewing the inside of her cheek. "I almost didn't come to Mumbai. A night before my train, I stayed up wondering if leaving Maa behind was the right call. I was guilty, she's done so much for me, and I felt…like…I was abandoning her."

There was a long pause. No rush to fill it.

"It's alright," Shreya finally said, "sometimes leaving is the first step to coming back stronger. Once you settle down, you can always bring Aunty here. Or give her the life she deserves from wherever you are."

Mihika nodded. "Your turn," she poked Shreya with her toe.

"Truth," Shreya said casually.

"What are you afraid of the most right now?" Mihika asked.

Shreya looked down at her hands. The candlelight flickered over her knuckles. "That I'll wake up ten years from now and still not know who I am without someone else defining me."

No one said anything for a few moments, but both Anagha and Mihika reached over, each squeezing one of her hands. Shreya offered a grateful smile. The words still echoed inside her, but in this moment, surrounded by quiet company, the fear felt less sharp. For now, it was enough.

Anagha leaned back. "Truth for me too," she said softly.

"Do you ever regret staying in this city?" Shreya asked this time.

Anagha's lips curved into a smile, tired but firm. It was more memory than expression. "Every monsoon," she said, "it was Kartik's favourite time of the year. There have been times when I felt guilty for enjoying the rains without him by my side, but…" She looked away blinking the tears. "But also no… this city is messy but it always gives you back. Maybe not what you wanted but what you needed."

Outside, a dog barked, a scooter came to life, and the rain turned softer almost like a lullaby. The electricity remained stubbornly absent. But inside that balcony, with three stories stretched across the floor and shadows bending kindly on the walls, something bright had already switched on.

●●●

The power returned in the early hours of the morning, announcing its arrival with the quiet whir of the ceiling fan. By then, the trio had dozed off in the living room, with shared quilts and borrowed cushions.

Shreya blinked awake to the faint hum of the electricity, disoriented for a second before realizing where she was. Beside her Mihika snuggled further into the quilt while Anagha slept upright against the couch with a book in her lap that Shreya didn't remember when she was reading.

Shreya checked her phone but it was switched off. She looked around the living room when she spotted the wall clock: 6:12 a.m. She padded towards the window. The rain had slowed down. Outside, the world had resumed. She saw a milkman pass by on his bicycle.

She brewed chai slowly, quietly. Enough for three. The gas clicked, the water hissed, and the cardamom cracked between her fingers. Familiar motions, newly comforting.

One by one, Mihika and Anagha woke up. Sleepy faces, out-of-place hair, no rush. No masks yet.

"Morning," Anagha mumbled, accepting her cup.

"I think I dreamed of Virat again," Mihika groaned, taking hers. Shreya shook her head.

They sat shoulder to shoulder in the living room, sipping chai as the mist caught the morning light. Pigeons flapped across telephone wires. Somewhere in the next balcony, a woman recited the morning prayers. None of them spoke for a long while. They didn't need to.

●●●

Mihika's fifth call finally convinced the locksmith to come to their place first. He arrived within half an hour. His helmet askew and smelling of cigarettes. In ten minutes, he replaced the lock to 4B and handed over two spare keys. "Foreign girls always forget the key," he muttered under his breath.

"We're from Dehradun and Ranchi," Mihika dead-panned.

The man laughed, pocketed cash, and rumbled off into puddles.

Shreya followed Mihika into their flat.

4B looked different now. It was still bare, but possibility shimmered beneath the bulb. Now it felt like something more than temporary.

Mihika reached for her phone. "I'm ordering curtains. This place needs to look and feel like home."

"Order the bright ones," Shreya said. Mihika was surprised. "We'll grow into them." Shreya finished with a shrug.

"I have spare fairy lights," Anagha offered from the doorway. Mihika and Shreya turned around. "And some poha." She showed them the plates.

"Then what are you waiting for, come on in." Mihika reached the door, taking a plate and pulling Anagha in, who couldn't help but chuckle at the former's excitement.

This was how things happened, Shreya realized. Not in grand declarations, but in borrowed fairy lights and shared breakfast and someone holding the ladder while you climbed. And sometimes, she thought, doors had to close so windows between hearts could open. And sometimes, at the other side of a locked door, waiting was the beginning of a home.

●●●

Two

The Arena and the Ancestry

Cs Rahul Srivastava

The sun dipped low over the battlements of Hastinapur, casting long golden shadows across the stone-paved courtyards. The great arena—crafted by artisans from the kingdoms of Anga, Chedi, and Panchala—stood proud and glistening in the saffron glow. Its granite steps were packed with citizens, noblemen, warriors, and scholars, all buzzing with anticipation.

The occasion was historic: the exhibition of martial skills by the princes of the Kuru dynasty.

From his elevated seat, King Dhritarashtra, blind yet dignified, sat beside Queen Gandhari and his half-brother, the wise Vidura. Bhishma stood just behind, a silent sentinel cloaked in silver armor. And at the corner of the royal balcony, almost blending into the carved stonework, sat Kunti—the silent queen mother. Her expression was unreadable.

Trumpets blared. Conch shells echoed. The arena hushed.

Out stepped Arjuna.

His gait was balanced and assured. Draped in white and gold, the son of Indra exuded effortless grace. He bowed to his elders, saluted the crowd, then notched a shimmering arrow onto his bow.

In moments, arrows flew. First into still targets. Then into moving ones. Then into impossibilities—threading rings in the air, splitting a fig leaf as it fluttered from a tree branch. Gasps rippled across the audience. Each feat was followed by polite claps from the Kauravas and thunderous cheers from the common folk.

Kripacharya smiled from the sidelines. "None can match Arjuna's focus."

"Not yet," Drona replied, stroking his beard.

And then, as if summoned by fate, the arena gates creaked open.

A charioteer's son stood there.

Clad in ruddy bronze armor that gleamed like captured sunlight, his face bore a strange serenity—half humility, half fire. A cloth band was tied across his brow. His hands were calloused, not from courtly rituals, but from battle.

He carried a worn bow. Simple. Scarred. Alive.

Gasps turned into murmurs.

"Who is he?"

"Another challenger?"

"Dare he walk barefoot among kings?"

The man stepped forward, bowed neither left nor right, and took his place at the mark Arjuna had vacated.

He said no words.

He simply let the arrows speak.

Seven targets. Seven arrows. Each fired before the previous one landed. Each hit dead center.

Then he raised his bow skyward and released one final shaft—it arched high, curved with impossible precision, and struck the golden bell on the far temple spire. The bell split silently into two, its echoes rolling across the arena seconds later.

Even Bhishma stepped forward.

"Remarkable," he whispered.

The crowd sat stunned.

Arjuna, face pale, looked to his teacher.

"Who is he?"

But before an answer could come, Duryodhana stood. His voice rang out like a battle horn.

"Let it be known: such skill deserves a crown. Let this man be declared King of Anga! I offer him my brotherhood!"

The crowd cheered. Servants brought a golden circlet. The priest raised incense.

But before the crown could touch the man's brow—a voice cut through the air.

"Stop!"

It was soft. Trembling. Yet it sliced through the air like a divine blade.

All turned.

It was Kunti.

The Truth Unveiled

Kunti stood alone, her white sari caught in the breeze, eyes wide but unwavering. For decades, she had lived with the weight of a secret buried beneath palace floors and maternal prayers. But now, in this sacred arena, under the eyes of gods and men, she could no longer be silent.

"That man," she said, her voice trembling yet clear, "is not a stranger. He is not a charioteer's son. He is my son.

My firstborn. The son of Surya. The elder brother of the Pandavas."

The arena erupted.

Some gasped, others cried out. Arjuna's bow fell from his hand. Bhima clenched his fists. Yudhishthira staggered as though struck by an unseen force. Duryodhana froze, his expression calcifying into disbelief.

Karna did not move.

"Say it again," he whispered.

Kunti stepped forward. "I bore you in secret, before I was wed. Afraid of disgrace, I sent you away. But I have never stopped searching your eyes in every corner of Bharat. You are Karna. My son."

Karna's breath caught. A thousand images surged through his mind—days of mockery, nights of longing, the sting of rejection, the silent pride of his foster parents, and the eternal ache of not knowing.

"Why now?"

Kunti's voice cracked. "Because today the world sees you. And if I let it go on, you would be raised as a challenger when you are a prince. You were never meant to walk in another's shadow."

Bhishma stepped forward slowly, like a mountain stirred to life.

"Then let it be known: Karna is Kunti-putra. Eldest son of Pandu's line. The rightful heir to the Kuru throne."

The priests murmured blessings. Scribes began to rewrite scrolls.

But Karna, overwhelmed, fell to his knees.

"Duryodhana," he said, turning toward the man who had raised him to prominence, "you gave me a name when the world gave me none. I owe you everything."

Duryodhana's face was tight with sorrow. "And yet... you are theirs."

Karna stood, eyes glistening. "I am yours. But I am also theirs. Let me be the bridge. Let me be the brother who unites, not divides."

The entire arena bowed their heads. In a single moment, truth had undone fate. The war had been paused—not by weapon, but by word.

Rise of the Eldest and the Path to Peace

The revelation shook the palace to its roots. Overnight, Karna was moved into the royal chambers once meant for Yudhishthira. Royal artisans embroidered his emblems anew—half-sun, half-wheel. Servants bowed deeper. Ministers greeted him with folded hands and trembling respect.

But Karna remained unchanged.

He refused opulence. He greeted his foster parents first, bringing them to the palace with royal honors. "You raised a prince without knowing it," he told them, touching their feet before the entire court. "And made him a better man than birthright ever could."

In private, he visited Kunti.

She knelt, tears flowing. "I do not seek forgiveness."

Karna held her hand. "I do not carry anger. Only longing—for the years that could have been."

It was Yudhishthira who proposed the next step.

"In spirit and blood, you are my elder, Karna. But the burden of kingship is not a gift. Will you accept it?"

Karna smiled. "No. Your mind is Dharmic. Your rule is just. Let me stand by your side—as sword and shield."

Thus began a new age. Karna was declared Senapati— Supreme Commander of the Kuru armies. His edicts brought sweeping change. Recruitment opened to merit, not caste. Soldier welfare camps were established. War ceased to be glorified—it was taught as a last resort, not the first instinct.

Arjuna became the master of military academies. He taught strategy, philosophy, and restraint.

Bhima oversaw the granaries and food security. Under his management, no child in Hastinapur slept hungry again.

Nakula revolutionized the cavalry; Sahadeva became the royal astrologer and agricultural reformer.

And Draupadi, as queen, led women's councils and educational reform, her voice echoing through law and literature.

The Kaurava Reconciliation

Duryodhana disappeared from public view for weeks. Rumors spread of revolt. But one morning, he emerged—no longer a prince, but a penitent. He arrived at court dressed in white, unarmed, and barefoot.

He bowed to Karna.

"I loved you as a brother," he said. "And I feared losing you more than any crown. But I see now—Dharma chose you to save us all."

Karna embraced him. "Let us write a new chapter—together."

The Kauravas and Pandavas, once rivals, now stood united. A new flag was designed—five arrows crossed with one sun above them. It flew over Hastinapur, and soon, over every allied kingdom.

Peace treaties were signed. Border disputes resolved. A conference of kings, the first in Bharat's history, was held in Kuru Sabha. Even distant tribes from the northwest and southern coasts sent envoys.

The world took note.

The age of iron had become the age of gold.

Legacy of Light and the Sunset King

Years passed like a gentle breeze across the plains of Aryavarta. Under the stewardship of the unified Kuru brothers, Hastinapur transformed from a kingdom of warriors to a beacon of civilization.

Markets flourished with goods from across the subcontinent—spices from the south, textiles from the east, bronze from the northwest. But it was not trade that made Hastinapur rich—it was the philosophy it gave to the world: that Dharma was not inherited, but earned.

Karna authored new laws: ones that elevated virtue above birth, service above pride. His famous decree, Karma is the caste, etched in granite, was read aloud in every village from Kashi to Gandhara.

He opened palace libraries to commoners. Every citizen, regardless of station, could learn astronomy, logic, history, and healing. Women were trained as diplomats. Farmers were consulted on harvest policies. And in temples, alongside priests, stood scholars and poets from every walk of life.

Krishna often visited—not as the god of war, but as a quiet observer. He would sit in Karna's courtyard under the neem tree, smiling.

"You were always the one," Krishna once said. "Not to destroy the old world—but to redeem it."

Karna chuckled. "You always knew. Why did you not tell me before?"

"I could only light the path," Krishna replied. "You had to walk it."

The Final Dawn

As years turned to decades, Karna's hair greyed. His eyes dimmed only in sight, never in purpose. One morning, as the sun rose over the Yamuna, he called his brothers.

They came—Yudhishthira in saffron robes, Bhima in his forest greens, Arjuna still carrying his bow more out of memory than need, and the twins in quiet reverence.

"I feel my time has come," Karna said softly.

"No," Arjuna said, grasping his hand. "Not yet. You still shine too bright."

Karna smiled. "Even the sun must set."

He rose, walked barefoot to the riverbank, and offered a final prayer to Surya. The villagers gathered quietly. Children held lotus garlands. Priests offered chants. The breeze was hushed.

As the light bathed his face, Karna closed his eyes.

And left.

Not with pain.

But with peace.

A World Reborn

Karna's body was cremated on the banks of the Yamuna. The pyre was lit not by royalty, but by five children—one from each caste—chosen for their compassion and courage.

His ashes were immersed where the rivers Saraswati and Yamuna met, under the first light of dawn.

Today, in this reimagined Bharat, history is taught not with wars and vengeance, but with stories of redemption and courage.

Children read about a man who defied rejection, who embraced truth over power, and who turned pain into purpose.

In the center of Hastinapur, where kings once held court, stands a marble pillar.

At its base is written:

"The warrior who chose unity over war, truth over silence, and brotherhood over pride—Karna, the Sunset King."

And it is said: every morning, the sun lingers just a moment longer above that pillar—as if bowing to its favorite son.

Three

The Missing Chapter

Mohika Bansal

Elina Verma had never believed in coincidences. As she stood behind the signing table at her book launch, a tremor passed through her fingers with each signature. Her debut novel, *murder at glance*, had garnered more attention than she could have imagined. But amid the bright lights, camera flashes, and compliments, a single line from a reader cut through everything.

"You wrote what only the killer would know."

At first, she smiled it off. Fans often said odd things. But when she flipped open the gifted copy she had just signed, a folded note fell out.

"You wrote what only the killer would know."

The words were handwritten, the ink slightly smudged, as if by a hesitant or shaking hands.

Her chest tightened. She looked around, but there was no one suspicious around.

Elina brought herself back, though her nerves tingled strangely. The last reader of the evening stepped forward—middle-aged, wearing an olive trench coat and a nondescript cap. His eyes, sharp and unusually steady, watched her without blinking.

"Elina Verma," he said, placing the book in front of her. "Your words are haunting."

"Thank you," she replied, uncapping her pen. "Who should I make it out to?"

The man didn't answer. Instead, he leaned in slightly and said, "That murder scene in chapter twelve... The red scarf, the cellar, the curtain folds—you wrote what only the killer would know."

Elina froze.

Her pen hovered above the title page, ink dotting the corner. "Excuse me?"

But the man had already turned. He slipped into the dispersing crowd and vanished through the exit without collecting the signed book.

For a moment, she sat still, her breath shallow.

"Elina?" Neha appeared beside her, sipping iced coffee. "You look like you've seen a ghost."

Elina shook her head and forced a chuckle. "Just nerves. Post-launch jitters."

The note stayed with her long after she returned home. Her apartment, a seventh-floor space filled with warm lighting and too many plants, usually comforted her. Tonight, it felt unfamiliar.

She sat at her desk, the note beside her laptop, and opened her email out of habit. Among the congratulatory messages and reader fan mails, one new subject line jumped out:

"Isha—Dalhog, 2014."

No sender name. No text body. Just a PDF attachment. She clicked it.

A scanned newspaper clipping loaded on her screen.

Girl Found Dead in Dalhog Estate — Case Remains Unsolved After 10 Years

Elina leaned in. The image was grainy—a young girl's face, blurred in monochrome. But the name chilled her blood.

Isha. Age: 10. Last seen wearing a red scarf. Found in the basement of an abandoned colonial home. Cause of death: strangulation. No suspects. Case closed as unresolved in 2015.

She reread the article three times.

The setting. The details. The scarf. The cellar. Even the way the body was covered—these were exact to her fictional chapter twelve.

But she'd made that scene up.

Hadn't she?

She called Neha immediately.

"Are you messing with me?" Elina asked, voice trembling.

"What? No! What happened?"

"I just got sent a real-life article about a murder that's nearly identical to a scene in my book. Same town. Same details. Even the red scarf."

There was silence on the other end.

"Elina…" Neha finally spoke. "Didn't your grandmother live in a town called Dalhog?"

Elina blinked. "No, she was in—wait." A flash surfaced. A long driveway. An iron gate. Crickets in the night. "I… I think we visited once. But I was really little."

"You said this was all fiction, right?" Neha asked carefully.

"Yes," Elina whispered, staring at the article. "At least, I thought so."

That night, she didn't sleep.

She sat in front of her manuscript, re-reading Chapter Twelve. She had written it in one burst, the scene fully formed in her head. The killer hides the body behind the wine barrels. Covers it with a silk curtain. Folds it thrice. The girl's hair is tied in a red scarf.

She remembered writing it. She remembered the candle flickering beside her as she typed. But now, as she read the sentences again, they felt foreign. Not hers. Like someone had whispered them to her in a dream.

At 3:17 a.m., she got another email.

From: Rivan

Subject: You Remember More Than You Admit

Body: "She cried for help. You heard her. But you were told to forget."

Her skin prickled.

Who was Rivan? And how did he know these things?

She opened her drawer and pulled out her old childhood photo album. Pages filled with birthday parties, vacations, school plays. One photo, loose and faded, fell out.

She turned it over.

"Elina & Isha — Summer, 2013."

She stared at the image.

Two girls. Her, unmistakably younger by a decade. And beside her, a girl with deep eyes and a bright red scarf.

Isha.

The photo slipped from Elina's trembling hands and fluttered to the floor. She didn't remember this picture being taken. Yet there she was, smiling with a girl who looked hauntingly like the one from the newspaper clipping. The name "Isha" was scribbled in childlike handwriting, unmistakably her own.

Elina stared at the red scarf around Isha's neck. Not just any scarf—it was patterned with gold embroidery, exactly as she'd described it in her book. A chill ran down her spine.

How could she have forgotten someone like Isha?

She picked up the photo, her hands clammy, and stared at it under the desk lamp. In the background stood an old colonial-style house. Ivy snaked across the walls, and two stone lions guarded the gate. The Dalhog estate.

"I was there," Elina whispered. "I knew her."

She flipped back through the album. Most pages were of her Delhi life. But in the middle, crammed between a birthday party and a Holi celebration, was a forgotten envelope. Inside were three photographs and a map. One photo showed her standing beside a rusted iron gate; another, a boy holding a slingshot. The third—

The third showed Isha sitting at a wooden table with a dog-eared book in her lap.

The title read: Whispers Beneath the Mango Tree.

Elina's breath caught. That book had inspired her to write The Red Widow. But how did Isha…?

She flipped open the map. Scribbled in a corner, barely legible, was a sentence:

"The cellar is beneath the mango grove. You promised not to tell."

Her head pounded.

There had to be an explanation. Maybe this was childhood imagination twisted by trauma. Maybe she had seen something back then and forgotten—suppressed it.

But why was it returning now?

And who was Rivan?

The next morning, Elina made a decision. She would go to Dalhog.

She didn't tell Neha. Just packed her bag, locked her flat, and boarded a train heading north. As the city slipped away, she tried to calm the whirlwind of half-memories and broken flashes—children running through tall grass, laughter echoing from empty halls, the heavy clang of cellar doors.

Six hours later, she stepped onto the cracked stone platform of Dalhog Junction. The air was thick with humidity and dust. A faded signboard swung lazily above her, its letters almost erased by time.

The estate was a thirty-minute walk, but she took it slowly, absorbing everything—the rustling trees, the quiet whispers of the wind. When she reached the iron gates, they were just as she remembered from the photograph.

Rusty. Majestic. Guarded by two stone lions, their faces cracked and worn.

Elina pushed open the gate with effort. The path to the house was overgrown. The house itself, once grand, now stood in silence—shutters loose, vines choking the windows. She stepped inside.

The floorboards creaked beneath her. Dust coated everything. Her footsteps echoed through the empty halls. The scent of damp wood and old secrets hung in the air.

She wandered room to room until she found it—the study with the fireplace, the winding staircase, the broken grandfather clock. And behind it, a door.

The cellar.

She hesitated.

Then she turned the handle.

The door groaned open.

The cellar was colder than she expected. The stone steps descended into darkness. She used her phone's flashlight. Cobwebs hung like veils, and the air was damp, metallic. Wine barrels lined the far wall, collapsed in some places.

She walked slowly, every step stirring dust.

Then she saw it.

A fold of faded red fabric caught on a splintered barrel.

Her breath hitched.

She reached for it—red silk, with gold embroidery.

The same scarf from the photo. From her book.

From Isha.

She turned and shone the light across the cellar.

And that's when she saw the carvings on the wall.

Childish letters scratched into the stone:

"Isha was here."

"Elina lied."

"Rivan watches."

Her hands trembled.

"Elina…"

She spun.

No one was there.

But she heard it—her name, whispered. Not imagined.

A presence.

She backed up the stairs and out into the main hall, heart hammering. As she stepped into the drawing room, a figure darted past the broken window.

"Wait!"

She ran outside, breath ragged, and chased the shadow around the side of the house into the mango grove.

There, beneath one tree, stood a boy. No older than ten. Barefoot. Dirty clothes. His eyes glowed with something ancient. Something knowing.

"Elina," he said.

She froze.

"Who are you?"

"I'm Rivan."

Her mouth went dry. "You're just a child."

"Not anymore."

He stepped forward. "You promised to protect her. But you forgot."

"I didn't know—I didn't remember."

"You blocked it. Like they told you to. But Isha never left. Not really."

He pointed upward.

"She's still here."

Elina looked.

There, tied to the branch above, was the same red scarf—fluttering in the wind, as if waiting.

"She knew too much," Rivan said quietly. "And they were afraid."

"Who?" Elina asked.

"The ones who used the estate. They came at night. Men with secrets. She saw them. And she told you."

Elina's vision blurred. Flashes returned—men in uniforms, a locked door, Isha crying.

"You told her it was just a game," Rivan whispered. "But it wasn't."

Elina dropped to her knees, clutching her head.

"I didn't know… I didn't mean to…"

"But now you do," he said. "And now, they know you remember."

He handed her a torn page.

From her own manuscript.

But the chapter number read: 13.5 — one she never wrote.

And at the bottom, in blood-red ink:

"The truth was never fiction."

Elina stood frozen in the grove, the tattered page trembling in her hands. The words written on it made her feel as if the ground had been ripped out from under her. How could someone have written this chapter? It was her voice, her style, even her peculiar metaphors. But she had never written a Chapter 13.5.

The lines were disturbingly specific—scenes she barely recalled herself. A girl being dragged down into the cellar. The words: "They took her because she saw the truth behind the curtain." And a final line:

"One will forget. One will disappear. And one will remain—watching."

Elina looked up, but the boy—Rivan—was gone.

She turned around, scanning the trees. The air had changed; the sun was dipping fast, bleeding orange into grey. A strange silence fell, broken only by the wind playing with the scarf tied to the branch. It unfurled for a moment like a warning flag.

She backed away and ran toward the house.

Her mind raced.

Who were "they"?

What truth had Isha discovered?

And why did someone want to hide it—badly enough to erase it from Elina's memory?

She spent the night at the estate. It felt reckless and unsafe, but somewhere deep inside, she knew she needed to face this place fully. There would be no answers if she fled again.

She locked the main door, pulled out a dusty mattress from a bedroom upstairs, and wrapped herself in a shawl. But sleep wouldn't come.

In the stillness, her phone buzzed.

A message.

Unknown Number:

"You went back. The book was never meant to remember. Now they will come for the writer."

She stared at the screen, numb.

A second message followed.

"Run if you like. But the cellar never forgets."

She turned the phone off and held it tightly, as if the screen might come alive and pull her in.

Outside, the wind howled against the windows.

At midnight, a loud clang echoed from downstairs.

Then silence.

Elina waited, heart pounding.

Nothing more came.

By morning, she had made a plan. She needed help. Answers. Proof that she wasn't going mad.

She took the scarf, the photographs, and the torn page and boarded the next train to Delhi. But she didn't go home.

She went to someone she hadn't seen in years.

"Tanishq Rao, Investigative Journalist."

That's what his dusty nameplate read.

He was a former crime beat journalist who'd gone off the radar after exposing a major political scandal. He and Elina had once worked on a short-lived podcast. He had a nose for buried stories.

When she showed up at his door, he blinked at her for a moment. Then he stepped aside.

"I figured you'd resurface when the past got loud," he said, leading her in.

"Did you ever hear of a girl named Isha Malhotra? Went missing in Dalhog, maybe fifteen years ago?"

He froze.

"Where did you hear that name?"

"She was my friend. I think. But... I forgot about her. Until now."

Tanishq lit a cigarette, hand shaking slightly.

"Isha's disappearance was buried. Never made the news properly. Her father was a clerk. Her mother... worked as domestic help in that estate before it was abandoned. There were whispers of child trafficking. Ritual abuse. Elite involvement. But no one followed it."

Elina felt her stomach twist.

"There's more," she whispered. "She told me something. When we were kids. I think she saw something—maybe someone—doing terrible things in that house. I wrote it, unknowingly, into my novel. And now..."

Tanishq studied her.

"What you're describing—it's not coincidence. It's extraction."

"What?"

"Memory extraction. Hypnosis. Trauma erasure. It's been used before. On witnesses. On whistleblowers."

Elina blinked. "That's not possible."

"Not legally," he said. "But for the right price…"

He pulled out an old file.

"She's in here. Isha Malhotra. Look."

A single black-and-white photo. Her school uniform. A police stamp. "Missing. Presumed runaway."

Elina touched the page. "She didn't run away. Someone took her."

Tanishq nodded. "And someone paid to make sure no one remembered."

That night, Elina received another message.

This time, a voice note.

She hesitated, then hit play.

It was her own voice.

But she didn't recall recording it.

"He told me to forget. He said if I ever remembered, they'd come for me next. I signed something. A waiver.

There was a man in white. He put wires on my temples. Isha screamed…"

She dropped the phone.

The note kept playing.

"…and then everything went black."

At 3 AM, Elina jolted awake.

Tanishq had set up his projector, scanning satellite images of Dalhog from a decade ago.

"There's something behind the estate," he said. "Look."

He pointed at a blurred satellite photo. A small structure, barely visible. Bunker-like.

"That wasn't there in the latest images. Either it was demolished—or hidden."

"What was it?"

"No idea. But if Isha saw what happened in that place, it would explain why someone went to such lengths to silence her."

Elina exhaled shakily. "I have to go back."

"No," Tanishq said sharply. "Not alone. Not again."

The next morning, they drove to Dalhog together.

But when they reached the estate, it was different.

The gates had been removed.

The house... burned. Still smoldering.

Ash, smoke, and twisted metal were all that remained.

Someone had torched the place.

Erased the last traces.

Tanishq cursed under his breath. "They're tying up loose ends."

Elina stared at the destruction, numb.

A shadow shifted behind a tree.

She turned.

It was the boy.

Rivan.

Untouched. Unbothered.

He raised a finger to his lips.

Then pointed to the ground.

They walked over.

Beneath the mango tree, half-buried in ash, lay a tape recorder.

Tanishq picked it up and pressed play.

A girl's voice.

Young. Clear.

"Isha Malhotra, age ten. This is my truth."

A pause.

"They said if I told anyone, they'd make me disappear. But I'm not afraid. Elina will remember one day. And when she does, please—find the locked room. The real one."

The recording clicked off.

The words from the tape echoed in the air like a curse:

"Find the locked room. The real one."

Elina and Tanishq stood in the charred remains of the estate, the mango tree casting long shadows as dusk settled in. Though the fire had devoured the building, something far older, far more sinister still lingered.

"We're not done here," Tanishq murmured. He crouched near the tree and brushed away more ash. Beneath it, brick. A corner of a trapdoor.

Elina knelt beside him, heart hammering.

"This wasn't in the original plans," she whispered.

They cleared the debris. Hidden beneath decades of neglect and now smoke, a rusted iron handle emerged. Tanishq gripped it with a cloth, heaved it upward. The door groaned open, revealing a narrow staircase spiraling into darkness.

Without a word, they descended.

The air turned thick, the temperature dropping with every step. The walls, lined with stone and timeworn planks, were damp and moldy. Their flashlight beams flickered over graffiti—chalk scrawls, tally marks, smeared red handprints.

At the bottom, a corridor stretched before them, branching into three doors.

The first was ajar. Inside, a makeshift medical room. Rusted tables. Chains. A cracked mirror. A broken typewriter with yellowed paper still in the roll.

Tanishq leaned in. "Read this," he whispered.

Elina took the paper. Her hands shook.

Subject EL-7 shows strong resistance to hypnosis. Memory suppression unsuccessful. Emotional triggers remain. Recommendation: isolation and aversion therapy.

She dropped the page.

"EL-7... That's me, isn't it?"

He nodded slowly. "Elina verma. The seventh subject. You were part of this."

She backed away, clutching her head. Fragments flashed—her being strapped to a bed, voices urging her to forget, and Isha's terrified eyes peering through a vent.

"I was part of their experiment."

The second room was colder.

Rows of old VHS tapes. Each labeled with names. Isha. Anay. Divya. Rivan.

Elina pulled out the one marked Isha – Session 6.

They found a player under the desk, miraculously still working when powered up by Tanishq's portable battery.

Static.

Then: a dim room. Isha, tied to a chair. A man in a white coat asked, "What did you see?"

Isha's voice was firm. "I saw the door open. I saw what you did to her. To Elina. I won't be quiet."

The man approached her. "Then we'll make you forget too."

The screen cut to black.

Then flickered back on.

This time: Elina. Younger. Pale.

She whispered, "I'll pretend to forget. So they stop. But I won't. I won't."

She looked directly at the camera.

Straight into future-Elina's eyes.

Elina stepped back, breath ragged. "They recorded our pain. Like… trophies."

Tanishq nodded grimly. "This wasn't just abuse. It was a program. Behavioural control. Memory erasure. Weaponized trauma."

The third door loomed.

Heavy. Bolted. Padlocked three times.

"The locked room," Elina whispered.

Tanishq pulled out a metal bar and snapped the first lock. The second and third took time. Sweat beaded their foreheads.

Finally, the door creaked open.

The air inside was stale—untouched for years.

And there, in the middle of the room, lay a child-sized bed.

Toys.

Drawings on the walls.

And a name scrawled in crayon: ISHA.

This had been her prison.

Elina stepped forward, tears rising.

Photos were pinned to a corkboard—blurry images of men in suits, envelopes, surveillance logs.

Tanishq began photographing everything.

Then Elina found a notebook. Isha's handwriting again.

If you're reading this, Elina, it means you remembered. I always knew you would. I tried to protect you by taking the fall. But you were stronger than they knew. This isn't just our story. This is how they've kept people quiet for years.

Don't stop now. Tell the world. Even if they come for you again.

Elina clutched the book to her chest.

"Isha..."

"She never made it out," Tanishq said softly. "But she left this behind for you. For justice."

Suddenly, footsteps.

Above.

Then descending.

"Run," Tanishq hissed.

They grabbed the tapes, the notebook, and fled through a side passage. A rusted ladder led them through a collapsed grate into the forest behind the estate.

Gunshots rang out.

They didn't stop running.

Back in Delhi, Elina hid in Tanishq's safehouse. They digitized everything—photos, recordings, testimonies.

Sent it to trusted journalists and activists. Days passed in a blur of fear and adrenaline.

Then, on the tenth day, Elina went live on a secure podcast stream.

She told the story.

Every piece.

Not just about Isha—but about the experiments, the erased memories, the manipulation of truth.

The story exploded across the internet.

Some called her a whistleblower. Others, a liar.

But survivors began to write in.

One woman from a boarding school in Himachal.

A boy from a juvenile center in Bhopal.

They remembered too.

Three weeks later, Elina received a package.

No return address.

Inside, a single photograph.

A girl, now a teenager, with eyes she'd never forget.

Isha.

Alive.

Smiling.

And a note:

"You remembered. I waited. I'm ready now."

The moment Elina saw the photograph, time stopped. Isha—older now, with streaks of defiance and sorrow in her eyes—was unmistakably alive.

"She made it out," Elina whispered, trembling.

Tanishq leaned over the photo. "This changes everything."

Elina stared at the note again. You remembered. I waited. I'm ready now.

"She was hiding," Elina realized. "All this time, waiting for someone to bring the truth to light."

It was no longer just about memory or justice—it was reunion. Resolution.

They traced the package's postmark to a remote village in Himachal Pradesh. Quiet, veiled in mist. They arrived under cover of darkness, following a trail of coded coordinates Isha had scribbled on the back of the note.

The final point was a hilltop cottage surrounded by tall deodars. As they approached, a lantern lit up on the porch.

And then, the door opened.

Elina froze.

It wasn't a dream.

Isha stood there, wrapped in a shawl, eyes wide, glistening.

"Elina," she breathed.

No words could prepare them. They simply embraced, dissolving into tears—years of pain, fear, and longing flooding the silence between them.

Later, by the fireplace, Isha poured everything out.

"I escaped the night of the fire," she said, voice brittle. "They thought I too burned. I saw my chance and ran."

She hid in a nearby orphanage for years, using a false name. Eventually, she met an old journalist who believed her story. He helped her disappear completely. "He died last year. That's when I started leaving breadcrumbs for you."

Elina clutched her hand. "Why didn't you come to me sooner?"

"They erased your memory. You weren't safe. But I never stopped watching. I followed your art, your books. The moment you published that story about a missing girl in a boarding school, I knew—you were remembering."

They sat in silence, two souls stitched together by pain, finally whole.

Back in Delhi, the world was shifting. Elina's revelations had sparked a wave.

The media called it "The Hidden Chapter Scandal."

Government bodies were forced to open inquiries into the orphanage's files. Survivors stepped forward. A few of the men from the tapes were arrested. One disappeared mysteriously.

A deeper rot was being uncovered—experiments, psychological manipulation, abuse under the guise of "behavioural research."

Some parts of the system tried to discredit Elina. But the truth was already out.

And Isha was the proof they never expected.

Elina and Isha began working with survivor advocacy groups. They launched an initiative called Project AINA —named after a child whose voice had been silenced in one of the sessions they'd discovered.

The Initiative offered therapy, legal aid, and most importantly, a platform for silenced voices to be heard.

Months later, Elina stood at a TED-style talk, facing a packed auditorium.

She began with a sentence that once haunted her: "Memory is not always lost. Sometimes, it's buried—because the truth would break us."

She paused, letting the silence breathe. "But I remembered. And in remembering, I found my voice. And my sister."

The crowd rose to their feet in thunderous applause.

After the event, Isha joined her backstage. They stood by the balcony, watching the sky burn golden with the setting sun.

"You ever wonder what would've happened if we never remembered?" Isha asked softly.

Elina nodded. "All the time."

"But I think," she added, "we were never meant to forget."

Isha smiled. "Not everything buried is meant to stay hidden."

They stood together—two survivors, two sisters—gazing at a future they carved from ashes.

A story once erased… now rewritten in fire.

Four

The Superpower Of Words

N. Thieyana

"Idiot, Good for Nothing Lazybones…What are you doing? Watching TV when semesters are coming up. See. If you become an unemployed goon don't come running to me. I won't give you a single paise.Idiot..Stupid" Rajan's loud voice could be heard even at the end of the street.

"No pa.." Ritesh started to explain.

"Oh. You have started arguing with me now. Just because you have started going to college doesn't mean you can talk back to me, stupid. Stupid.."

"No nga..He was studying the entire day. He was just relaxing." Rajan's wife Meenakshi started saying.

"Relaxing. From what? Is it so difficult to sit under cool air and study. Look at me. I have been standing in scorching heat the entire day regulating traffic. As Traffic police I have been doing it for past 35 years. What will happen if I decide to relax? You and your kids will be begging in the street."

"Relax, Relax, my foot…" Mr. Rajan was muttering to himself.

The time was around 6'o clock in the evening and it was 10 minutes since Rajan entered his house in which around 8 minutes was spent yelling at his son and wife.

The remaining two minutes he was muttering angrily to himself.

Just then Rajan's oldest daughter Shreya tried to tip toe silently towards the door. She almost reached the door when the booming voice reached her, "Where do you think you are going dressed like that? You look like a clown. Go change and for God's sake remove your awful makeup."

Shreya's eyes brimmed with tears; her voice shook when she started to argue but Rajan shut her up even before she started. "Listen to me and don't argue. You come from a good family and you are going to be married soon. Remember that. I wont let anyone question your upbringing at your in-law's house. So, dress properly. Go."

Shreya went back to her room quietly. In fact, the house was so quiet except for the angry muttering of Rajan complaining about government, his boss and neighbours and thousands of other stuffs that it was difficult to believe that there were other family members living in the same house as Rajan.

Meenakshi was in due course subjected for another round of shouting for the inferior taste of the filter coffee she served Rajan.

Just when Rajan seemed to calm down the door bell started ringing.

On answering the door, Rajan found Kavin and Mohammad, two of Ritesh's best friends at the door.

"As if one wastrel is not enough there seems to be a conference of wastrels. What are you guys doing here? Don't you have subjects to study? The youngsters today roam around, doomscroll, daydream instead of doing anything useful" Rajan's mouth was spewing harsh words at the speed of bullets from a machine gun.

But Kavin and Mohammad were unfazed as they were used to Rajan since they were in elementary school.

Mohammed started saying politely, "Uncle, we came for a group study with Ritesh. There are some tough subjects that we have to crack together."

"Group study. You think I was born yesterday. All you guys do in the name of group study is to discuss about

movie stars and cricket players. Giving you guys education is waste of a parent's money, time and energy. Now go to his room but be sure that I will come and check on you guys every 15 minutes", Rajan commanded.

The boys moved away without saying anything. Rajan looked out of the apartment just to see that his neighbour has parked his scooter three inches within Rajan's parking lot that seem to aggravate Rajan to no end. He started spewing hateful words about his neighbour and his irresponsibility for the next 15 minutes.

So far we could deduce that Rajan's favourite past time is to yell at anyone within his eyesight. Ritesh always wondered about this characteristic of his father. To be truthful his father was hardworking without any bad habits, a loyal son to his parents and a good father and husband. He provided them with whatever they wanted and seemed to care about their welfare. But everything becomes meaningless when his yelling start. As the kids grew older this trait of their father seemed to confuse and suffocate them. "If you can't say something nice why tell them at all"..right..

The next day evening Rajan's household was oddly quiet. Even though Rajan's two-wheeler was standing in the parking lot, there was not a peep from their house. Ritesh on returning from his college, found this unnerving. He wished his father was shouting which would indicate that everything was normal. This silence was ominous. With certain trepidation Ritesh opened the door only to see a very odd scene.

His father was lying on the sofa looking blankly at the roof and his mother was sobbing quietly nearby. Shreya's eyes were so round that it was almost comical. Ritesh slowly approached his mother and asked her whether there is any emergency. Slowly between sniffles she told him that there was some kind of altercation at Rajan's workplace which may or may not result in his suspension. If he is suspended so near to his retirement all the allowances and settlement money which they are banking on for his sister's marriage may be in jeopardy.

When Ritesh tried to talk to his dad all he got was a rude reprimand from Rajan asking him to mind his own business. Somehow the situation at home seemed to get worser so Ritesh decided to go to his father's workplace and try to find out what exactly happened.

Without telling his father, Ritesh approached Kumar, who was working as a clerk in his father's office and was also the only friend of Rajan. Mr. Kumar told him that on one particularly busy day, when there was peak traffic, a car got broke down in the middle of the road which resulted in an epic traffic jam. Rajan who was trying to regulate the traffic as the traffic police in duty got so mad. He approached the vehicle and started berating the driver with rude words.

The driver was a mechanic who was test driving his client's car when it broke down unexpectedly and even though he tried to explain his situation Rajan in his true style was yelling at him non-stop. A friend who was accompanying the mechanic has discreetly filmed the entire episode in his mobile phone and have filed a defamation case against Rajan.

Now Ritesh was conflicted. Asking his father to apologise is out of question and at the same time the mechanic has taken his father's ranting as a direct hit against his self-respect. Ritesh was desperately thinking of a way out of this sticky situation only to end up with unbearable head ache.

On the weekend Ritesh, Kavin and Mohammad were seen walking the crowded streets of the less affluent part of the city. They showed up at the door of the mechanic's shop asking for Rahim. Instead, Rahim's friend Sundar accosted them and started interrogating them harshly. When Ritesh stated the reason for their visit, Sundar went ballistic.

"So, you have come along with your friends to seek vengeance for your father. Is that it? Do you want to fight with us? It will be a losing battle and we will thrash you all into pieces? Do you hear me?" Sundar was almost mad with anger.

"You posh kids think that with your fluent English and higher education you can lord over us. You think you could command us like dogs. Let me tell you, this is our area and we are law unto ourself. We could literally make you disappear.", Sundar was shaking his hands in a threatening manner all the while an excited crowd was forming around them.

Rithesh spoke calmly," No brother. We came just to talk to Rahim. We don't have any ulterior motives."

But the crowd was too hyped up and was raring for a fight. Each one was shouting their own opinion about the atrocities of affluent people and the people who are in power. How they are subjected to untold miseries and unfair laws because of some preconceived notion that all the people from poorer part of the city are hoodlums and rowdies.

The situation was fast getting out of hand and Mohammed and Kavin were scared. They tried to pull Ritesh from that place. But they were truly and completely boxed in by the angry mob.

A silent man was observing all this from the inside of the mechanic shop. Suddenly he stood up and asked everyone in the crowd to disperse. The crowd was shouting encouraging words to him.

"Don't worry Rahim. We will protect you. This is our locality and we protect each other. Don't be afraid", an elderly man told Rahim with much gusto.

Rahim calmly asked everyone to go back to their own works telling them that he is perfectly capable of looking after him by himself. When Sundar tried to argue with him, Rahim asked him to calm down and let him take care of the situation.

When the crowd disbursed with much grumblings and disappointed sighs the boys breathed a sigh of relief.

Rahim looked at them and simply said,' There is a hotel two streets over. There we can talk, Come with me."

They reached the hotel and occupied a seat at the back of the hotel. After ordering a cup of tea for all of them Rahim simply stared at the boys.

Ritesh started speaking," Sir, we are all first-year computer Engineering students. My name is Ritesh and I am the son of Mr. Rajan against whom you have filed a complaint."

Rahim asked, "So you have come to threaten me to get back the complaint. Is that it?"

Ritesh's eyes were wide and he was shaking his head no quickly.

"No, No. I simply came to talk to you about my father and the reasons behind his actions. "

Ritesh took a deep breath and continued," On that particular day, my dad was chewed out by his superior officer who was twenty years younger than him in front of all other employees just for no reason at all. It may be because my father is an honest official who never accepted bribe and this has always irked his higher officers. My father suffers from high blood pressure. He has fixed my sister's marriage with a respectable family who are demanding exorbitant dowry amount. He has very recently borrowed a lot of money to cover my fees just a few months ago. "

Rahim cooly asked," So you have come as your father's mouthpiece with all your sob stories so that I would drop the charges?"

"I just wanted to apologise on my father's behalf and wanted to tell you that he is not a bad person. "

Just then Mohammed started to talk, "In fact uncle is a kind-hearted person who doesn't know how to show his love. He actually believes in tough love where he shows his concern in the form of yelling. A few years back, house owners were reluctant to let us rent their house because we are muslims. But uncle stepped in and vouched for us and made sure that we get a nice house at an affordable rent."

Kavin nodded his head," My father died when I was very young. When my mother struggled to pay school fees, uncle quietly paid it and never talked about it to anyone. At one point when I was ready to dropout from the school, he stopped me and made sure that I continue my education come what may".

Ritesh continued, "I am not saying what my father did was correct despite numerous reasons that pushed him to act that way. I just want you to understand that he is just an insecure, overworked and depressed government servant. In our country our friends and neighbours would be willing to protect us from physical harm or perceived insults. They may even loan us amount and protect us from financial ruin. But the moment they see us struggling with our mental health they give us wide berth. The men in our country are taught to manage their mental pressures through liquor addiction or through impotent rage that results in yelling etc. women resort to tears or self-destruction. All I ask is to empathise with my father's condition and understand that what he did was not out of hate or with any intention to cause harm."

Rahim remained silent. Mohammed said softly," I know words have the power to hurt us most than any other sharp weapon but I beg you to think of his yelling as same as the yelling you might get from your own father."

Rahim stood up and said," Well I wouldn't know. Would I? I have never had a family. I am an orphan." He went to the bill counter paid for their tea and just left.

The next day evening, Ritesh was studying in his room when Rajan quietly came in and sat near him. He didn't talk for a few minutes and that shocked Ritesh. When he looked at his father questioningly Rajan just smiled.

After a few minutes he started speaking, "That boy has dropped the charges so I am not going to be suspended."

Ritesh was overjoyed and said," That's good news pa."

Rajan thoughtfully nodded and started to talk in a quiet voice. "That boy came and met me and told what you and your friends did for me. I am so grateful to you and so very proud of you. Instead of resorting to violence or arguments you guys acted in a very matured manner. I sincerely apologised to that boy for my rude behaviour."

Rajan continued," You are completely right, Ritesh. Whatever problems or tensions in my job I brought it to the house and made you all miserable too. I couldn't control my anger and frustrations and I took it out on you all. That could not and should not be easily forgiven. Yet I will apologise to your mother and you kids for making your life so unbearable for all these years. I promise I will start meditating and take proper counselling to control my anger issues."

Ritesh felt over the moon and hugged his father tightly.

"Appa this is actually the good news. You are willing to change and that is the best outcome that could come out of all these confusions. What Rahim did was a really good deed. Can I ask him to come to our home for lunch some day pa?" Ritesh asked eagerly.

"Sure, Sure..that's a nice idea" Rajan agreed.

Five

From the Unknown, He Grew

Parveen D

Ladies and gentlemen,

Let me take you on a journey. Not across continents or through the pages of history, but into the heart of a story that could belong to any one of us. A story of beginnings, of struggles, of quiet battles fought not with swords, but with silent strength. A story not carved in headlines, but written in the unnoticed moments of life.

It begins, as most stories do, with a dream.

A family, carrying more hope than belongings, moved across state lines. They came with nothing but a belief — that maybe, just maybe, a better life was possible. They didn't know the language. The streets were unfamiliar. Even the sky seemed like a stranger.

And yet, they moved forward.

In the middle of this family was a boy. Small, wide-eyed, untouched by the weariness in his parents' eyes. He played, he laughed, he studied up to the 9th standard with joy that no currency could buy. And though poverty crept into the corners of their home, his parents never let it enter his heart.

But children are not blind. They feel what is not said. He saw their sacrifices — quiet, daily, unspoken. And one summer, while other kids played cricket or slept in, he made a choice. A choice that would shape him.

He became a water can delivery boy. No license. No roadmap. Just willpower.

Under the scorching sun, with the weight of water on his shoulders and purpose in his chest, he delivered hope — not just hydration. Every trip was a message: "I see you, Amma. I see you, Appa. This is my thank you."

That was his first job — not on a résumé, but etched in his soul.

But this family, they were made of something different. They didn't come to survive. They came to rise. And that boy? He was their rising sun.

As he stepped into the 10th standard, life intensified. It was a year that could shape his future. So he woke up at 5:30 AM, took crowded buses across the city, and returned home only when the stars had replaced the sun.

Those buses weren't just transport — they were his second school.

He listened. He observed. He learned not just algebra and history, but humanity. He studied people. Their faces. Their silence. Their joy. Their despair. And slowly, unknowingly, he became a student of life.

He passed the 10th with grace — not just in marks, but in maturity.

Then came a summer of laughter. Time with his sisters. A rare pause in a life that had already demanded too much, too soon.

As he moved into the 11th and 12th standards, his world expanded again. New friends. New lessons. New emotions. He learned about love — not just from textbooks, but from experience. A relationship spanning nearly seven years, grounded in trust and tested by distance.

They met only twice a year.

Yes — twice.

Because they both knew something that many forget in today's world of scrolling screens and shallow reels — love is not about quantity. It's about quality. About meaning. About patience. They stayed in touch, but chose not to get lost in endless chats or calls. Because they believed in preserving the spark. In protecting their dreams — and each other.

They chose depth over dopamine.

They knew that in a world addicted to instant gratification, the most precious things are the ones that grow slowly.

And then came college.

Not by passion. But by expectation.

He didn't choose his course — he inherited it from society's idea of success. Because where he came from, degrees weren't decorations. They were lifelines. College wasn't an exploration — it was a necessity.

Still, he made the most of it. Rose to become the department secretary — a role many admired. But admiration is not the same as fulfillment. Behind the applause, he felt a strange emptiness. A dissonance between what he was doing and who he truly was.

So he did something unheard of.

He chose to fail. Deliberately.

Not because he couldn't pass. But because he wanted to feel the weight of failure. To understand its taste. To experience what so many fear — and learn that it does not destroy you. That failure, when embraced, becomes a teacher far more powerful than success.

And when he rose from that, he rose wiser. Stronger.

Eventually, he graduated. The first in his family to do so. A moment that should have felt like a trophy. And it was — but not for him. For his parents. For the generations that came before him, who never had the chance.

And amidst all this — there was one dream that never left him.

The Royal Enfield GT 650.

It wasn't just a bike. It was a symbol. Of freedom. Of power. Of possibility.

He saw it first in the 12th standard. Back then, it cost nearly three times his entire college fee. But he didn't laugh at the dream. He nurtured it. Quietly. Faithfully. Every rupee he earned, he saved for that machine. It became his secret promise to himself.

But life… has a way of testing how deeply we mean what we say.

His family needed him. And without a second thought, he gave them everything he had saved.

Not because he had to. But because family comes before fantasy. Because some dreams can wait — but our loved ones cannot.

Still, the universe didn't forget him.

At 21, he bought himself a Royal Enfield 350.

Not the GT 650 — but a dream nonetheless.

And here's the thing.

He bought it with his own money. No loans. No help. No co-signer. No credit card EMI.

He walked into the showroom alone.

He signed the papers alone.

He took the keys alone.

And he rode away — not with noise, but with pride.

That bike was not just a vehicle. It was a victory.

A medal for the boy who carried water cans.

A symbol for the student who studied strangers on buses.

A reminder for the teen who dared to fail.

A reward for the man who gave up his dream to lift up his family.

You see, ladies and gentlemen, this story is not about becoming a millionaire.

It's about becoming a man.

It's about resilience. Grit. And growth.

It's about understanding that sometimes, you have to walk alone — not because no one cares, but because your path is meant to be walked by you.

It's about realizing that silence doesn't mean weakness.

That humility doesn't mean invisibility.

That strength is not in shouting your story, but in living it.

And maybe this is your story too.

Maybe you're the one waking up at 5 AM while others sleep.

Maybe you're the one carrying dreams in your heart while carrying responsibilities on your back.

Maybe you've failed — not because you're weak, but because you were brave enough to try.

If that's you — know this:

You are powerful beyond measure.

You don't need applause to validate your journey.

You don't need likes, reels, or viral views to prove your worth.

You are growing — even if it's quiet.

You are winning — even if no one sees it.

You are riding forward — even if the road is long.

You are enough.

And just like the boy who grew from the unknown, you too will rise.

So, don't wait for permission to chase your dreams.

Don't wait for a crowd to start your journey.

Don't wait for the perfect time — there is no such thing.

Start now.

Start with what you have.

Start where you are.

Because every legend began as a nobody.

Every story began in silence.

Every hero once walked alone.

So ride — not to impress, but to express.

Not to escape, but to arrive.

Not to chase attention, but to honor your growth.

And remember…

Your journey may not be on maps.

Your struggle may not be on feeds.

Your story may never go viral.

But that doesn't make it any less extraordinary.

From the unknown, he grew.

And so can you.

Thank you.

Six

The Whispering Guest

Kishore Kumar

In an age long past, around the late 9th century, when the world was still largely untamed and villages clung to life at the mercy of nature, lay the remote settlement of Oakhaven. On a thick, foggy night, Almiran, the village head, walked cautiously through the dense forest with two villagers, Kai and Soren.

Almiran, in his forties, was a tall, imposing man, his face marked by the years of hardship he had faced. Kai, a lean man in his thirties, with nimble hands adept at setting traps and a quiet intensity in his eyes, walked slightly ahead, his breath visible in the cold night air. Soren, also in his thirties, with a broad build, a rough beard, and a scar running across his cheek, trudged beside them, his eyes darting nervously around. They each carried a dead pig over their shoulders, their muscles straining from the weight. Almiran held a wooden fire torch high, the flames flickering wildly in the wind, casting erratic shadows around them. The surrounding trees appeared like twisted, skeletal figures, their branches outstretched like claws reaching for something unseen. The ground underfoot was dry, and every step seemed to echo a quiet, unsettling crunch.

"We've wandered this forest since dawn... now it's almost midnight," Soren said, looking concerned. "Something about this forest feels... wrong."

"Why can't we find animals nearby anymore?" Kai muttered, his voice filled with frustration. "It's getting harder to hunt."

"It's like everything's against us," Kai added, his voice low with desperation. "With no rain, the fields are drying up, and now we can't even hunt in this forest."

Almiran's grip on the torch tightened. "Keep moving," he commanded, his voice low.

But then, he heard it, a faint whisper, carried by the wind. It was so soft, like a distant murmur, that he almost dismissed it as the rustle of leaves. But the sound persisted, growing slightly louder. Almiran paused, turning his head toward a large, twisted tree whose bark was blackened and peeling like ancient skin.

"What was that?" Kai asked, sensing Almiran's hesitation.

Almiran didn't answer immediately. Instead, he took a few steps toward the sound, raising the torch higher to pierce through the thick fog. The flickering light created strange, shifting shadows that seemed to dance around the tree. As he got closer, he used the torch to clear the mist and saw something hidden behind the tree, a small, dark statue, reaching up to Almiran's knee, half-buried in the dirt.

The statue was carved from a peculiar black stone, its surface covered in grime. It had a twisted, grotesque shape with hollow eyes that seemed to stare directly at Almiran. For a moment, he felt the air grow colder, but he dismissed it as a trick of the mind. The whispers grew louder in his ears, now more like a low hum, but he couldn't make out the words.

Kai and Soren moved closer, trying to see what Almiran was looking at.

"What is it?" Soren asked, a hint of fear in his voice.

Almiran, still staring at the statue, replied, "I've never seen anything like it before."

The words felt heavy on his tongue. A strange compulsion gripped him.

"We should take this with us," he declared suddenly.

Kai looked uneasy. "Are you sure? It feels... strange," he said, his voice faltering. Kai and Soren exchanged a nervous glance, their eyes questioning Almiran's sudden decision to carry this unsettling find.

"We need to know what it is," Almiran insisted, reaching down to lift the statue. As his fingers touched its cold surface, a shiver ran up his arm, almost as if the statue was vibrating. He quickly shook off the sensation, handed the torch to Kai, and lifted the statue into his arms.

A strange, unyielding obsession flickered in Almiran's eyes as he cradled the dark figure. "Let's go," he commanded.

With the statue held firmly in Almiran's arms, they continued their trek out of the forest. Kai and Soren walked a little behind, their shoulders still burdened by the pigs, but now also by a growing unease. The whispers that seemed to follow Almiran were imperceptible to them, yet an unsettling quiet had descended upon the woods around them. The fog seemed to thicken, pressing in, making the already dark forest feel even more foreboding.

Almiran, however, walked with a focused intensity, his eyes fixed on the path ahead, seemingly oblivious to their apprehension. The group rejoined the other hunters at the forest's edge. Several villagers were already there, gathered around a crackling bonfire, warming themselves as they waited anxiously. Seeing Almiran and the others emerge, they quickly picked up the deer and other hunted animals they had laid out and rushed forward.

"Where have you been? We were getting worried!" one shouted.

"Wait... What's that?" another asked, pointing to the dark figure Almiran was carrying.

"We found it in the forest. We're bringing it back to the village," Almiran replied, his voice steady, but a strange look flickered in his eyes.

Kai, seeing the animals they carried, gave a wry smile.

"Remarkable. It seems you had more luck than us tonight. We thought we'd be the only ones with anything to show."

A burly hunter, with a dead deer still on his shoulder, smiled and patted it.

Yet even amid the chatter, a strange discomfort lingered. Their eyes occasionally flicked toward the statue, but no one spoke. Still, they followed Almiran's lead. Once they left the forest and reached the village's back entrance, the villagers, still curious and a little wary, helped Almiran carry the statue to what remained of an old, crumbling shrine. It was a small, roofless structure, its broad base made entirely of packed earth, not stone, visibly worn and broken by time. It stood right there, at this entrance.

Almiran carefully placed the statue directly onto the soil, its dark form settling unevenly against the ground of the crumbling shrine.

"It's already late, Almiran," Kai said, trying to draw him

away. "Everyone's waiting, hungry."

Everyone turned to leave, but Almiran remained, staring at the dark figure with a strange, almost obsessive look in his eyes. Soren gently tapped his shoulder, bringing him back to his senses. Together, they finally left the shrine and walked towards the village fires.

Unseen by them, as the last of their footsteps faded, the black stone statue subtly shifted on the uneven ground, settling deeper and more firmly into the soil.

The villagers gathered around the fires they had built near their huts, cooking the meat they had hunted, singing, dancing, and sharing stories in celebration. Almiran sat with his wife, Elara, and his young son, Finn, who was about 12 years old. Almiran's eyes occasionally drifted toward the direction of the statue, a flicker of hope crossing his face. Kai smiled, watching his young daughter, Lyra, who was about 8 years old, twirl and laugh in the firelight, her joy infectious. For a moment, everything seemed normal, the villagers were lost in their momentary happiness.

The following morning, Almiran's sleep was restless, filled with oppressive nightmares of a parched, desolate land and the hollow whispers echoing in his ears. His eyes flickered open and shut, his head shaking, his face contorted with fear. He suddenly woke up, his breath catching in his throat. The phantom sounds of the nightmare faded, and immediately, the unusual scent of wet earth, of life returning, along with the soft drumming of rain against his hut, filled his senses.

A sense of disbelief washed over him, followed by a surge of desperate hope. He quickly got up and ran outside and stepped under the eaves of his hut to find the villagers celebrating in the downpour. Overjoyed to see their happiness, Almiran spotted Kai already soaked and enjoying the rain with his daughter, and nearby, his son, Finn, was also laughing and splashing in the puddles.

"Father!" Finn shouted, waving excitedly, his face bright with unburdened joy.

Almiran's wife, Elara, joined him, a warm smile on her face.

 "Finn, come here or you'll catch a terrible flu!" she called out playfully before turning to Almiran, her eyes glowing with a profound happiness.

"It's been too long since we've seen our people truly happy, Almiran."

Almiran placed a hand on her shoulder, both of them soaking in the miraculous sight and the steady, relentless rain, a true gift after the long drought that had softened the cracked earth. "I sensed this, Elara. Hereafter, everything will be good for us," he said, a newfound hope in his voice.

As the villagers danced, their bare feet sinking into the pliable soil, their joy was unburdened, a relief after the oppressive drought that had plagued them for so long.

After a few hours, the people, drenched but joyous, gathered around the statue, which still stood at the back entrance of the village, at the crumbling shrine, offering small tributes of food, flowers, and trinkets. Villagers believed that the statue brought luck to their village.

Stepping forward, Almiran declared,

 "As I believe, our sorrows will wash away with this rain. This is our god, who brings wealth to our land and our people."

The villagers cheered, their spirits high as they reveled in the rain.

Unseen by their celebrating eyes, the black statue, once covered with grime, now appeared to shimmer with a strange, almost slick sheen as if it was freshly awakened. The rainwater, instead of pooling, was eagerly drawn into the parched ground around its base. The rain softened the soil, allowing the statue to settle deeper and more firmly into the land.

Over the next few months, the villagers busied themselves with their daily activities. They worked joyfully in the fields, seeding and cultivating their crops with renewed enthusiasm. Men ventured into the forest for hunting. The nights were filled with lively celebrations, as the villagers partied and danced, often reveling in the steady, soothing rain.

However, a troubling change began to unfold.

Villagers slowly began to realize the rain grew heavier and more relentless with each passing day, flooding the crops. Cattle fell sick and died mysteriously. The villagers grew ill from unrecognizable sickness, Kai's daughter, Lyra, among them, her bright spirit slowly dimming. Many villagers' minds became clouded with fear and anger. Friends turned against each other; violence erupted, staining the village with blood, and many accused the statue of bringing this madness.

They had pleaded with Almiran to remove the accursed thing from the shrine — to throw it deep into the forest or destroy it — but he had steadfastly refused, never allowing anyone near it. Amidst the chaos, Almiran continued to visit the statue constantly. Each night, he remained awake, his eyes hollow, haunted by the persistent whispers.

One stormy night, a desperate wail echoed through the village.

Almiran, his eyes bloodshot from sleepless nights, rushed out into the pouring rain to find Kai kneeling, holding his daughter's lifeless body in his arms, soaked to the bone, his face twisted with anguish.

"Help me! Please, someone, help!" Kai cried, tears mixing with the rain on his cheeks. Almiran approached, his heart heavy. He touched the child's neck, feeling the absence of life. His hollow eyes, accustomed to months of detachment, remained calm with no immediate emotion. The villagers gathered, their faces pale and fearful.

"It's that cursed statue!" someone shouted, their voice laced with terror.

"It's brought death upon us!"

"Why did you bring that here, Almiran?" another accused, their voice trembling with anger. "Our children are dying because of that thing!" a third cried, pointing a trembling finger at the shrine. "I swear, I even saw the statue move by itself!" a fearful villager whimpered, stepping back from the crowd.

The whispers in Almiran's head grew louder, an insidious chorus, overriding the villagers' lamentations and pleas.

"How dare you!" Almiran raged out at the villagers and continued,

"That statue saved us from the drought! It brought us rain!"

"But at what dreadful cost?" Soren fired back, his voice raw with grief.

"Look around, Almiran! We've traded hope for ruin —
our lives for slow death! The fields are flooded,

and our people are dying!"

Kai, his face full of grief, turned to Almiran, his voice
shaking with rage.

"It's only a matter of time before it's your child!" he
screamed.

"We have followed you without question, Almiran,
through drought and hardship," Soren added, stepping
forward.

"But this... this is not the leader we know, the man who
cared for our village. This time, for the sake of our very
survival, we will make our own decision."

Kai, still clutching his daughter, his voice breaking,
declared — a momentary pause hanging heavy in the
storm-filled air —

"We've had enough. We're getting rid of that thing
tonight, whether you agree or not."

All those words pierced through the fog in Almiran's
mind, and his hollow eyes came back to life. He swept his
gaze across the faces of the sick, coughing villagers, the
festering wounds of unknown sickness visible on some.
He saw the raw grief on Kai's face and the lifeless form

of his daughter. His eyes then fell upon his own son, Finn, a flicker of true fear igniting within him.

He remembered the simple, honest joy of the villagers even in the depths of the drought, a happiness untainted by this insidious 'gift'. A wave of profound shame and bone-deep fear washed over him, shattering the unnatural calm. For a moment, he looked at the direction of the statue, and a sickening clarity, devoid of any former reverence, filled him.

"You're... you're right," Almiran rasped, the words barely forming, his voice thick with a sudden, overwhelming grief.

"The whispers had drowned out your voices. I couldn't hear my own people. I am… I am sorry. Forgive me."

He knelt, the heavy rain washing over his contorted face, tears mixing freely. Then, with a deep, shuddering breath, the air filling his lungs as if for the first time in months, his shoulders straightened, not just with resolve, but with a fierce, almost violent determination, his voice now a raw roar that cut through the downpour.

"This ends tonight! We will destroy that monstrous thing!"

The villagers erupted in cheers, their faces lighting up with relief to see Almiran finally coming back to his senses, now they were ready. But first, there was a solemn duty to perform. They gently carried Lyra's small body to the cold, rain-soaked earth, burying her amidst their tears and vows of vengeance.

Kai wept openly as he gently lowered her, whispering a final, tearful goodbye. Almiran approached, placing a heavy hand on Kai's shoulder.

"We will not let this happen to any more of our children, Kai," he vowed, his voice hoarse with fierce determination. Then, with grim resolve, Almiran stepped forward, seizing one of the shovels. "Take your shovels, let's bury this evil tonight!" he commanded, his voice raw with conviction.

They began their march through the storm. The relentless rain poured down, and lightning flashes periodically illuminated their path, revealing the dark, menacing silhouette of the statue looming in the distance. Even from afar, its ominous presence intensified with every step, a silent, obsidian monolith mocking their grim purpose.

Finally, they reached the crumbling shrine, standing before the statue. Up close, the rainwater streamed down its dark surface, catching the lightning in grotesque ways, making the statue appear to writhe and its once-revered features twist into a permanent, malevolent sneer. The villagers stood transfixed, their faces pale, staring at it.

Kai, his face a mask of grief, rage, and tears, stepped

forward first, his hands shaking, and wrapped them around the base of the statue. He pulled with all his strength, but the statue wouldn't budge.

"Help me lift this thing!" Kai shouted, straining against the statue.

The villagers rushed to his side, pulling and pushing, but it wouldn't budge. Refusing to give up, they seized their shovels and digging bars, trying to pry it loose from the ground.

As they dug around the base, they discovered something horrifying. Thick, dark tendrils of stone spread out from its base like veins, anchoring it firmly into the earth. The tendrils were sinking deeper and deeper, entwining with the land itself.

A man, his eyes drawn to the statue's hollow gaze, screamed,

"This isn't a god! It's a demon!"

He stumbled back in horror, dropping his digging bar as primal terror seized him.

A heavy whisper, thick and cloying, slithered directly into Almiran's mind, a voice only he could hear, trying to reclaim its hold. He squeezed his eyes shut, pressing his hands against his ears as if to physically block it out, but the insidious words coiled around his thoughts. For a moment, the old confusion threatened to return, but then, fueled by the rage of his village's suffering and the sight of Kai's daughter, a newfound, unyielding strength surged through him.

He straightened, his face hardening into a mask of fierce determination, his resolve unshakeable. "You can't consume me! Not anymore!" Almiran roared, his voice cutting through the storm.

The remaining villagers, though shaken but resolute, kept digging. As they dug intensely, one of them stumbled, and his shovel slipped, striking his foot. Blood gushed from the wound, splattering across the statue's surface.

The moment the blood touched it, the black stone seemed to shiver, absorbing the crimson liquid instantly. An unnatural cold swept through the air. The statue shuddered violently. A low, grinding sound accompanied its grotesque expansion as it swelled and stretched upward, becoming impossibly more imposing and terrifying, with spider-web cracks spreading across the wet ground around it.

One of the villagers sank to his knees, utterly defeated, his face pale with despair, and began to laugh — an unhinged, chilling sound that quickly warped into a mad, booming cackle.

His eyes wide and vacant, he shrieked,

"The land is his! And we... we are his feast!"

and continued to laugh, a chilling, unhinged sound that echoed through the storm.

The whispers returned, echoing in everyone's minds, growing louder, more piercing. These whispers then converged into a single, sinister, hollow voice that erupted from the statue, vibrating through their very bones:

"...HUNGRY."

Seven

Shadows and Sunlight

Varthini Parthiban

Part 1: The Life That Changed

The morning sun pierced through the thin curtains of the 8th-floor apartment in Bangalore. Tanya stood silently in the kitchen, stirring the boiling milk as the news played in the background. The anchor's voice faded into the white noise of her thoughts.

"Thara, come on baby, wake up!" Tanya called, her voice echoing down the hallway. She adjusted the flame and walked to her daughter's room.

Twelve-year-old Thara groaned and turned in her bed. Tanya gently brushed the hair from her forehead and whispered, "Rise and shine."

Thara opened her eyes and smiled sleepily. "Five more minutes, Amma."

Tanya smiled back but with eyes that had forgotten how to sparkle. "Your five minutes turn into fifteen every day."

Back in the kitchen, Rohan scrolled through emails on his tablet, sipping the tea Tanya had placed before him.

"There's a release next week," he muttered, not really speaking to anyone.

Tanya nodded. That was her husband, Rohan. Responsible. Loving. Provider. Father. But slowly, unknowingly, they had started living parallel lives, orbiting around their daughter like two distant moons around the same planet.

Rohan was the kind of man every woman hoped to marry—caring, respectful, hard-working. Tanya had loved him deeply once. She still did, perhaps, but it was buried under layers of frustration and resentment.

●●●

Twelve years ago, everything had seemed perfect. They married after a two-year relationship, dreaming of a life filled with love and adventure. Within a year, Tanya gave birth to Thara. That was when the cracks began.

Tanya had always been ambitious, a coder with flair and a love for building things from scratch. But motherhood came with an invisible rulebook—one that demanded all of her, every moment, every breath.

With no parents nearby and no help available, she quit her job. Rohan's salary was enough to keep them afloat.

She told herself it was just for a few years. Five, maybe. Until Thara was in school. Then she would return to work, to her identity.

But when that time came, the world had moved on. Her field had evolved. The gap in her résumé widened into a chasm. Interviews became rejections. Rejections turned into silence. And slowly, Tanya turned into a ghost of her former self.

Her days revolved around laundry, cooking, and helping with Thara's homework. She smiled at neighbors, nodded at Rohan's updates, but inside, she was hollow. Unseen.

Rohan noticed something had changed. But he thought it was just exhaustion. "Tanya, take a spa day," he'd say. Or, "Order food tonight, don't stress."

He thought love was providing comfort. But all Tanya wanted was to feel like a person again.

•••

The fights began as whispers, then escalated into thunder. Every now and then, Tanya would explode. "I have no life!" she'd yell. "I don't even know who I am anymore!"

Rohan would reply, "You think I have it easy? I work 12 hours a day for us!"

Thara, who used to hide under her blanket during their

fights, had grown to quietly weep into her pillow.

One night, in a particularly heated argument, Tanya shouted, "Maybe we should just get divorced if we're this unhappy!"

There was silence.

Thara stood frozen at the doorway, her face pale. She ran to her room and slammed the door. Tanya's chest rose and fell rapidly, realizing what she had said. Rohan stared at her in disbelief. That night, Thara cried herself to sleep, terrified her family would fall apart.

●●●

A week later, Rohan sat beside Tanya as Thara was at school.

"We can't fight like that in front of her," he said.

Tanya nodded. "I didn't mean what I said. I was just... tired. Angry."

"She's hurting. We need to be better."

So they struck a deal: no fights in front of Thara, no harsh words. A quiet truce, if not peace.

In an attempt to help, Rohan registered Tanya at a library nearby. "You always loved books," he said, placing the card on the table.

Tanya was touched. It wasn't a solution, but it was a start. A small gesture that felt like a hand reaching out across a widening gap.

At the library, Tanya found comfort. The smell of old books, the hush of the room—it was like stepping into her past. She started visiting regularly, even making casual conversations with other readers.

One such reader was Arjun, a middle-aged professor who loved classic literature. They bonded over books, laughed at each other's recommendations, and slowly, Tanya's laughter returned—at least inside that library.

●●●

One day, as Thara was returning from school early due to a half-day, she spotted her mother outside the library.

Tanya was laughing heartily, brushing hair behind her ear as Arjun said something animatedly. Her eyes glowed, her face bright with amusement.

But to Thara, the scene looked different.

A strange man. Her mother laughing like that.

Her heart sank.

●●●

Thara stormed into the house and waited. When Tanya

entered, humming softly, her daughter erupted.

"Who was that man, Amma?!"

Tanya, startled, blinked. "What?"

"I saw you laughing with him! Outside the library!"

Tanya's smile vanished. "That's none of your business."

"You're cheating on Appa!" Thara screamed.

Tanya's eyes flared. "Enough, Thara! Don't talk nonsense!"

The room felt heavy. Anger and pain hung in the air.

Rohan walked in minutes later and Thara ran to him, tears streaming down her face. "Appa... Amma is with someone else."

Rohan looked at his daughter, then at his wife. The moment hung, suspended like a breath held too long.

But instead of fury, his voice was calm. Firm.

"Thara. Don't say such things without knowing the truth."

"But I saw—"

"I trust your mother. And you should too."

Tanya blinked rapidly, her eyes moist. She didn't expect this.

Rohan walked to her, held her hand gently, and said, "I may not have understood you, Tanya. I thought I was doing enough. But maybe... I wasn't."

Tanya burst into tears. Years of frustration, loneliness, and longing came pouring out. "I felt invisible," she sobbed. "Just a mother. Not me. I forgot who I was."

Rohan hugged her. "And I should have helped you remember. I was so caught up in work... I forgot you had dreams too."

Thara, confused and emotional, ran to her parents. "I'm sorry, Amma... I didn't mean to..."

They embraced, a silent agreement passing between them. No more silence. No more assumptions. Only understanding.

Part 2: A Room of Her Own

In the weeks that followed, the house grew quieter—not with tension, but with peace. There were fewer raised voices, more paused conversations. The air wasn't always heavy anymore.

Rohan made small changes—he came home early at least once a week, helped Thara with her school projects, and on Sundays, he made breakfast. Messy omelets and burnt toast, but Tanya appreciated the effort more than the result.

He even surprised her one evening by updating her résumé with a new layout and font.

"I found a few re-entry programs for women with career breaks," he said gently, handing her a printout. "Let's try again. This time, we'll try together."

Tanya stared at him, stunned. A part of her wanted to believe. The other part was afraid to hope again. But she took the papers anyway.

"I'm not expecting miracles," she said. "Just... something that's mine."

"I know," Rohan replied. "And you deserve it."

That night, for the first time in months, Tanya slept with a light heart.

● ● ●

At school, Thara began to feel better too. The tension at home had affected her more than she realized. Now, with her parents' renewed warmth, she found herself smiling more, studying better.

But the incident with her mother still weighed on her. She had judged too quickly. She hadn't asked. She hadn't listened.

One evening, as she sat with her mother folding clothes, Thara looked up. "Amma, I'm sorry."

Tanya stopped folding a T-shirt and turned to her. "For what, ma?"

"For thinking... badly of you. That day."

Tanya smiled, not with pity, but understanding. "You were scared. I was too harsh." Thara looked down. "Is that man your friend?"

Tanya nodded. "His name is Arjun. He teaches literature. We just talk about books." Thara gave a small smile. "He made you laugh. I hadn't seen that in a while." Tanya chuckled. "That's because I hadn't laughed in a while."

Thara reached for her mother's hand and held it. "I like it when you laugh."

That night, Tanya sat with her old laptop, the one she hadn't opened in years. The keys felt foreign at first. But as she typed, something inside her began to flicker. A familiar spark.

She registered for a free coding refresher course. Rohan helped her schedule a quiet corner of their home as her "study space." It wasn't much—just a table, a chair, and a shelf—but it was hers. A small island of purpose.

She began waking up earlier, spending a couple of hours on practice modules before Thara's school routine. Some days were hard—Thara needed help, groceries ran out, the power failed—but Tanya pushed through.

One evening, when she cracked a tough problem after three days of trying, she shouted with joy. Rohan and Thara came running, thinking something was wrong.

"I did it!" Tanya grinned, pointing at the screen.

Rohan clapped. Thara gave her a high-five.

"You're cooler than my math teacher, Amma!" Thara giggled.

●●●

Weekends became lighter. They started going to Cubbon Park again, something they hadn't done in years. Rohan packed a small picnic one Sunday. Tanya brought her books, and Thara brought her sketchpad.

"Why do you draw so many trees?" Rohan asked.

Thara shrugged. "Because trees don't leave."

Tanya and Rohan exchanged a glance. That one sentence said so much. Later that night, Rohan sat with Thara while Tanya rested.

"You know, when you grow up, you'll have tough days

too," he said. "But no matter what, don't bottle it up. Talk. Ask. Understand."

Thara nodded slowly. "I didn't understand Amma's sadness."

"Neither did I," he said, softly. "But we're learning. Together."

●●●

Months passed. Tanya completed her course and even volunteered for a small coding project with a local NGO. It didn't pay much, but it gave her confidence. She even gave a small talk at a women's meetup, sharing her journey of returning after a long break.

As she spoke to the group—some nodding, some teary-eyed—Tanya realized that identity wasn't always a straight road. It bent, paused, and sometimes, disappeared completely.

But it could also return. In whispers, in moments, in code, in applause.

Rohan and Thara waited outside after the talk. When she stepped out, Thara ran to her. "Amma! You looked like a movie heroine!"

Tanya laughed. "I was sweating the whole time!"

"You were glowing," Rohan added. "And I was proud."

She blinked back tears. The woman she was five years ago would have never believed this moment.

●●●

One night, as rain fell softly against their balcony windows, Tanya looked through old photos on her phone. The early days of marriage. Thara's first birthday. Trips, celebrations, then a long gap.

Photos without smiles.

Then, slowly, new ones appeared. Of the library. Of Tanya at her desk. Of Rohan burning toast. Of Thara's tree sketches.

She created a folder called "Reborn."

As she stared out the window, sipping coffee, Rohan joined her. "What are you thinking?" "That I'm not just someone's mother or wife anymore," she said.

"You were always more than that," he replied. "I just didn't remind you enough." She turned to him. "We forgot each other for a while, didn't we?"

"We remembered in time," he whispered.

She rested her head on his shoulder. Thara walked in, curled between them without a word, and the three sat quietly, the storm outside no match for the calm inside.

●●●

Epilogue

A year later, Tanya started her own blog, "Mothers Who Code." She wrote about restarting, failing, and learning. The blog gained followers. Women across India wrote to her.

She didn't chase the corporate ladder anymore. She created her own.

Thara, now thirteen, gave a speech at school about resilience. She ended it with, "My mother is my hero. She fell, paused, but never stopped."

Rohan sat in the audience, his eyes moist.

And Tanya, watching her daughter beam from the stage, smiled.

This time, her smile reached her eyes.

Eight

Of Love, Guilt, and Ghosts

Praveen Ramesh

We're moving to a different place all of a sudden. I'm in 8th grade and I have lots of friends here. I'm going to miss them a lot. I'm scared of the new school and new people. How will I make friends there? Do new friends like noodles? What kind of cartoons do they watch? Ah, I'm going to be in serious trouble.

At least I hope my mom spends more time with me. She's been sending me to lots of classes lately besides school. There's barely any time at home. I'm really tired of these classes and I hate them. But Mom wants me to go. Mom used to sleep with me, hug me tight, tell me stories, and I'd fall asleep very well. But recently, she's stopped sleeping with me. She says I've grown up. She's busy with work even at night. I hate this. I only spend nights at home and I can't even spend time with her.

Does she feel sad about it too?

My dad, on the other hand... I never saw his face until this year. Mom said Dad was working far away and couldn't come here. There's no picture of him in our house. People usually have wedding pictures, but my parents don't. Mom said Dad would be here this year. She had a couple of calls with him. She even bought him clothes and gifts. One day, he came over. We had dinner. He looked shocked seeing me. I was happy… but I didn't know how to express it. What should I have said? "Love you, Dad"? Was that too much? Maybe "How are you? Did you miss me?" I didn't know. So I stayed silent. He didn't say much either. After dinner, Mom and Dad went to a room privately. It sounded like they were arguing. I went near the door.

"Why didn't you say anything about the kid?"

"I thought you would love her."

"Of course I like her. But we're meeting now to understand each other. You should've told me about your life—about the marriage and the kid…"

Hearing this confused me. What were they talking about? Then I heard something break. Did he break it? Did he throw something? Dad stormed out of the house angrily. Mom came out. I asked her what happened. She didn't even look at me for a few hours. Then she said, "Dad was angry I didn't tell him more about you. He didn't know about your schooling or the fee issues. I hid it because I didn't want to make him worry. But he was sad. He accidentally broke your toy by stepping on it. I'll buy you a new one. Sleep well, baby."

It didn't make any sense. Didn't they talk about me all these years? He didn't say a word to me but got into a fight with Mom?

Mom is amazing. She's been with me all these years—not Dad. He should've talked to me. Spent time with me. That conversation didn't sit right with me. Are they hiding something? Mom said Dad would come to the new house in a day or two. When he does, I'm going to ask all the things I've kept in my mind.

We reached the new house. Behind it was a dense forest. Each house was far apart—you literally needed a vehicle to visit the neighbors. The place had no air, dry leaves, and complete silence. No sound. No birds.

All the trees and plants were bare. The weather was dark, yet oddly warm.

While we were unloading things, my toy ball fell and rolled into the foggy area behind the house. Mom went to get it but didn't return for a while. After a few minutes of silence, I called out:

"Mom... Mom..."

She came back. "I couldn't find the ball, honey. Can you go look for it? I have more things to move in." So I went into the fog. It was thick. I couldn't see anything. No sound. No wind. No trees. After walking a bit, I saw a round object in the distance—my ball! I ran towards it. As the fog cleared slightly, I saw a huge, dead tree. No leaves. Its branches looked like arms trying to catch someone. The hollow in the trunk resembled a face. The bark was scarred. It was terrifying—like something from a horror movie.

But my ball was right there. I ran fast, picked it up… and for a second, I swear the tree moved toward me. A breeze passed, making me shiver. I sprinted back to the house.

When I returned, Mom had already arranged most things and was cooking my favorite noodles. The house smelled amazing. I was excited.

When I grabbed the remote to watch TV, I saw a gift box.

"Mom, what's this?"

"It's for you, honey. Open it."

I opened it—it was the cute dress we saw last night at the supermarket. I loved it. I hugged Mom.

"Thank you, Mom!"

"It's okay, honey. Do you like it?"

"I love it, Mom!"

"Can you wear it for me?"

I ran, changed into it, and showed her. She was happy. We sat down to eat noodles and watch cartoons. I asked her:

"Mom, will you spend more time with me?"

"I will, honey. I'm always with you. I love you."

"I love you too, Mom."

Just then, the phone rang. Mom picked it up. No one answered. Network issue?

A few minutes later, another call came. Mom picked it again. "Is the work done?"

Mom replied, "Not yet. I'll finish it soon and call you back. She's listening—cut the call. I'll call you shortly."

"What's happening, Mom?"

"Nothing, honey."

Her face didn't look right. She looked sad. But when I looked at her, she smiled.

Another call came. This time, I said, "I'll pick it."

I answered.

No sound... then a voice.

"Honey, it's me."

It sounded like Mom. But she was right in front of me, watching TV. The light from the screen flickered on her face, but she didn't move at all. "Honey, it's me. Mom."

What?

"Baby, it's me. That's not Mom in front of you. I'm upstairs. Run. Don't stay there. Run!"

I froze. If Mom is upstairs... who is this?

"Mom... Mom?"

She slowly turned her head. She was wearing a mask. She stood up slowly... holding a knife in her hand.

I screamed and ran upstairs. As I ran, I heard a voice from a room to the right:

"Baby, don't go up. It's not me upstairs. Go somewhere else. Don't stay still!"

Confused and terrified, I ran to the left and locked the door. She knocked on the door:

"Baby, open the door. I brought your favorite noodles. It tastes so good."

"Baby, your favorite cartoon is about to end. Please open the door." "Baby… please open. I miss you. I want to hug you so tight." There was a door to escape, but it was locked. I searched for the key. "Baby, open the door. It will be quick…"

I found a key, but it wasn't for the door—it opened a box. Inside were pictures of Mom and Dad. A wedding photo.

Mom had hidden this all along.

But the man wasn't the one who visited us.

"That's your father in the photo, honey."

"Then who came to our house?"

"Open the door, honey. I'll tell you."

I kept looking. I saw pictures of Mom with another man—her boss. "Mom... is he your boss? Are you in a relationship with him? Then... he's not my dad?"

"Yes, baby. I'll tell you everything. Open the door. I'll show you your real dad."

I threw the photo frame. The glass broke. Inside was another key. I used it to open the other door.

It wasn't a room.

It was a cell.

The door vanished behind me—became a wall. The walls had drawings of the tree I saw earlier. There was a tiny window in the door like a hospital for the mentally ill.

I saw the mask Mom wore. I picked it up.

Suddenly... I lost control of my body.

I couldn't move.

Something forced me to wear the mask. I sat down beside myself... who was watching cartoons.

"Mom, come sit with me. Let's watch cartoons."

I wasn't me anymore.

I was Mom.

On the screen, my reflection wasn't mine—it was Mom's. I was inside Mom's body.

I passed out.

When I woke up… I knew everything. I was Mom. I had killed my daughter. The man I loved didn't want her. And I… I chose him. I'm not a mother. I'm a monster.

In that moment, all the pain and love my daughter had felt came rushing into me like a storm. I felt every tear she never cried, every hurt she kept inside, every little hope she held on to. Her voice, her fear, her longing— they all became mine. I wasn't just seeing her memories— I was completely lost in her love and pain.

Something was making me feel the love and pain my daughter experienced—over and over.

I picked up a knife.

I stabbed my throat.

When I opened my eyes… I was stuck on a tree. It had me tied, eating my skin and drinking my blood.

"Why are you doing this to me? Just kill me."

"You're doing this to yourself."

"What?"

"You're trapped in your own guilt. I'm not real. You're imagining me. You're torturing yourself."

I opened my eyes.

I was in a cell for the mentally ill.

I cried. I slept. But when I closed my eyes…

It began again.

I was my daughter. Again.

I felt everything she experienced—her love and her pain. It started again.

It never ends.

Until I die.

Nine

Where The Map Went Silent

Shiv Bhowmik

Part 1: The Error in Ink

The envelope had no address, no label—only a wax seal pressed so deep it looked bruised.

Rudra found it lying on the porch railing of his government guesthouse in Shimla, as if placed there by a hand that didn't want to be seen. The seal bore the old Survey of India insignia—retired decades ago. He hadn't seen that crest since his training days. It shimmered faintly, as though it remembered being relevant.

He picked it up. It was heavy, textured like the bark of a tree that had grown in silence. Rudra turned it over in his palm, frowning. Even the weight felt personal, like the envelope knew what it was interrupting. He hadn't seen a physical memo in years. The department had switched to digital notices long ago. But this—this was stubbornly analog.

He tore it open with his thumbnail.

Inside were three things:

A single-page letter written in a typewriter's fading font.

A folded map of Northern Himachal Pradesh.

And a one-way rail ticket to a station called **Kaalgaon**—a name he'd never heard, even after a decade in cartography.

The letter was brief:

To: Field Officer Rudra Thakur

Subject: Revalidation Survey – Section R7 (Kinnaur Sector)

A field discrepancy has been reported in the R7 grid. The last verified mapping was in 1987. No official updates since.

*Proceed to Kaalgaon Station and locate **Gridpoint R7-32B**. Confirm presence or absence of settlement. Report findings directly.*

Note: This assignment is analog-only. No satellite recon. No digital logs. Carry compass, paper, and sketch tools.

Travel safe.

Chief Cartographer – Archives Cell

Rudra reread it. Then once more.

He looked at the map next. It was worn, detailed, and smelled faintly of eucalyptus. A red dot marked **Gridpoint R7-32B**—somewhere beyond Kalpa, on a narrow foot trail that split away from the known villages like a vein forgotten by the body. **The red ink used for the dot had bled slightly, like it had been pressed too hard—or perhaps wept.**

He boarded the 4:42 AM train from Shimla under a fog that felt sentient. The platform lights flickered like a hesitant thought. His backpack was heavier than usual— not because of the tools, but the feeling in his stomach, dense and sour. Something about this journey didn't sit right. It wasn't just the outdated order. It was the tone of secrecy—as if he were stepping into a space meant to be forgotten.

By noon, the train veered east, out of signal zones, out of familiar valleys. The stations grew stranger—places without names, just painted numbers on stone markers. He fell asleep somewhere between two tunnels and woke to silence.

Outside the window: nothing.

No people. No station sign. Just **KAALGAON** written in faded paint on an arched metal gate, its letters nearly erased by time.

The station was deserted.

No chaiwala. No porters. Not even the stray dogs that made their kingdom along Indian tracks.

Rudra stepped down. His legs ached from stillness, his breath short not from altitude, but anticipation he couldn't explain.

There was a small wooden booth labeled Station Master, but the shutters were drawn. A cobwebbed bell hung from the roof, untouched.

A dirt path led upward into the forest, steep and veined with moss. The air was thinner here, **and tasted like old prayer books**. Rudra adjusted his bag, took out the compass, and began walking.

Two hours later, he reached the trailhead—a sliver of flattened grass marked by a hand-painted sign:

"To Shillak Village – 3 km"

Below it, etched crudely in chalk, were two words:

Or Further.

He frowned. That village name—**Shillak**—wasn't on his map. Not in any archive. Not even in the oldest census data he'd reviewed during training.

He made a note in his journal:

Trail forks north-east. Unrecorded. Slope moderate. Forest density: high.

No sign of other travelers. Atmosphere: still, but not silent.

Because the forest wasn't silent.

It **breathed**.

Bird calls. Leaves shifting like whispered arguments.

And beneath it all—a low hum. Mechanical, rhythmic, impossible.

He turned around once. Just to be sure the path home still existed. It did.

But it already felt like a memory.

By dusk, he saw rooftops.

Stone. Sloped. Weathered to ash.

A dozen houses huddled together like survivors of some old avalanche. Smoke curled from a single chimney.

He approached slowly, boots crunching gravel that felt too brittle for its age. No signs of electricity. No phone towers. No wires. And yet, the place didn't feel abandoned.

It felt... paused.

From the far end of the village, a figure emerged.

An old man, wrapped in a brown shawl, eyes sharp as bird claws. He stared at Rudra with something between recognition and mourning.

"You came late," the man said in crisp Hindi.

Rudra blinked. "I—sorry?"

"We expected you last monsoon," the man said, gesturing toward the houses. "But time runs strangely here."

"I was sent by the Survey of India," Rudra offered, showing his badge.

The man didn't even glance at it.

"We know," he said, and turned. "Come. The others will want to meet you before dark."

"Others?" Rudra asked, but followed anyway.

As they walked, Rudra noticed something strange.

The houses were not weathered in the same way. Some had modern bolts on old wooden doors. Others had solar panels that looked unused for decades. A few had shoes—**his brand of hiking shoes**—resting by the steps. Dirty, torn, but unmistakably modern.

His skin prickled.

Inside one of the larger houses, ten people sat in a circle. Young. Old. Middle-aged. All with the same **quiet eyes**.

And when they saw Rudra, **they all smiled.**

Like he was expected.

Like he was one of them.

He didn't sleep well that night.

The cot was soft, but the dreams were jagged. Faces from old textbooks. His mother's voice calling his name from a train platform he couldn't find. A map unrolling endlessly, its edges curling into smoke.

At midnight, he sat up and lit the oil lamp left on his desk. He opened his journal.

Inside, on the next blank page, was a sentence written in handwriting that looked like his:

You have always been here, Rudra.

The map was never meant to remember you.

His fingers trembled.

He looked out the window.

The village was gone.

Only mist remained.

Part 2: The People Who Never Left

Rudra didn't remember falling asleep.

He remembered the lamp flickering, the strange sentence in his journal, and the village outside his window fading into mist. But after that, nothing. Morning arrived without light—just a soft grayness seeping through the cracks in the wooden shutters. Kaalgaon had returned, like a shy animal reemerging after a storm.

Smoke drifted lazily from a distant chimney. The same old woman from the previous evening swept her porch with a twig broom. When she looked up and met his gaze, she nodded—not like a stranger might, but like a neighbor who had known him for years.

He returned the nod. "Namaste."

"You slept well," she said, her voice brittle with age but threaded with calm.

"I'm not sure I did."

She smiled faintly. "That's the only kind of sleep we get here."

At the center of the village, Deven Bhatt waited for him—same shawl, same stillness. A kettle boiled gently on a blackened stove beside a stone bench.

Rudra sat across from him. The tea smelled of cloves and something older, something harder to name.

"You didn't tell me your name," Rudra said.

Deven poured the tea slowly. "You knew it once."

"I don't think I did."

"Memory is soft here. Like chalk left in the rain."

Rudra accepted the cup, letting the steam rise between them. "How many people live in this village?"

Deven stirred his own tea with a twig. "More than you'll count."

"And how many were born here?"

Deven smiled at that, but it didn't reach his eyes. "Maps love answers. But villages like this… they prefer echoes."

Rudra looked away. A rusted sign hung on the nearby wall—once a government plaque, now defaced with red chalk. The original inscription had faded, but scrawled below it were three crooked words:

WE REMEMBER DIFFERENTLY.

Rudra spent the afternoon walking.

There was no road beyond the village, only a network of footpaths that doubled back on themselves like veins trying to escape their own origin. The trees here whispered in unfamiliar rhythms. His compass spun slightly when held too long in one direction.

In the far corner of the settlement stood a structure newer than the rest—a wooden building with polished beams and smooth floors. It looked like it had been built recently, yet its windows bore the dust of decades. No one stopped him as he approached. No one followed. But he could feel them watching.

He stepped inside.

It was a **library**—but not of books. Of journals. Hundreds of them.

Each one bound in cloth and shelved with precision. Small brass plates adorned their spines, each engraved with a name and year:

Neel Roy – 1972

Ranjan D'Souza – 1979

Vikram Mehta – 1969

Arunava Pal – 1985

Then, about halfway down the aisle:

Rudra Thakur – 2023

His stomach dropped.

He pulled it from the shelf with trembling hands.

It was filled.

Every page covered in handwriting that mirrored his own. Maps, sketches, notes—entries he hadn't made yet. Observations from days that hadn't happened. Conversations he hadn't had.

On one page was a sketch of the old man, Deven Bhatt, labeled **Guide – unverified origin.** Another page described the weather outside that very morning, down to the exact curl of the mist.

He shut the journal, breath shaky.

From across the room, something creaked. A warped mirror stood at the far wall, framed in old metal. Rudra approached slowly.

His reflection stared back at him.

But it wasn't him. Not quite.

The man in the glass looked… older. Grayer. The beard lined with silver. The eyes duller, the mouth resigned.

He stepped back.

That night, Deven joined him by the fire again.

"You saw the library," he said.

Rudra didn't respond.

"There's comfort in being remembered," Deven added. "But it can also be a kind of cage."

"Why me?" Rudra finally asked. "Why this place?"

Deven looked into the flames. "Because you stopped trusting what you couldn't measure."

"I was sent here," Rudra insisted.

Deven smiled. "Exactly."

He couldn't sleep.

At midnight, the journal on his desk rustled in the still air. He opened it.

A new entry had appeared, written in his hand:

She will arrive tomorrow. Don't call her by name. She doesn't remember yet.

Leave the compass by the water trough.

Time moves differently for everyone.

The next morning, Rudra stood at the well before dawn. Mist clung to the stones like skin to bone.

She came walking through it—drenched, wide-eyed, clutching a government-issued knapsack like it was a life raft. Her hair was tangled. Her boots were caked with mountain mud.

She stopped at the trough. Her eyes landed on the compass placed beside it.

She picked it up.

And then, as if pulled by a string she didn't know existed, she looked up.

A sharp pang bloomed behind Rudra's ribs— familiar and wrong, like déjà vu dressed in the wrong clothes. For a heartbeat, he thought he'd spoken to her before. Or dreamed her once.

Their eyes met.

Rudra didn't speak.

She didn't either.

She just nodded—gently, the way people nod to old stories half-remembered.

That night, Rudra wrote again:

Name: Ananya Sen

Assignment: Revalidation Survey – Gridpoint R7-32B

Date of Arrival: Not confirmed. Compass recovered.

She does not yet suspect she is home.

He paused.

Then wrote one last line:

Tomorrow, I will forget this again.

Part 3: The Ink That Doesn't Fade

Rudra sat at the edge of the library, his journal open on his lap.

It was evening—though in Kaalgaon, time never truly settled. There was no dusk in the conventional sense. Only a slow graying of light, as if the village exhaled and dimmed its own lantern. The rooftops dissolved into mist. Footsteps whispered on gravel.

The villagers moved like shadows with memory. None hurried. None lingered.

He turned the page.

There was a sketch of **Ananya**, drawn in his own style—though he had never made it. In the image, she stood beside the well, speaking to someone Rudra didn't recognize. Above the sketch, a new line of handwriting had appeared:

Tomorrow, she will ask where the road leads. Don't lie. Just ask if she remembers which direction she came from.

He closed the journal slowly. His fingers left faint impressions on the page, as if the paper could absorb uncertainty.

Because something was happening to his memory.

Moments slid into each other. Events arrived before they happened. And when he closed his eyes, he sometimes saw the village from above—**as if he were the map itself**.

That night, he wandered beyond the usual trail, past houses shuttered in sleep. A soft blue glow blinked ahead—faint, electrical, misplaced.

It came from a narrow building tucked behind two willows.

A faded board outside read:

KAALGAON POST OFFICE

Inside, the room smelled of dry ink and unopened truths.

There were no lights, yet he could see everything clearly. **Pigeonholes lined the walls**, each one filled with old, yellowing envelopes. Some were sealed. Others had split open from time and silence. Every envelope bore names he had seen in the library:

Neel Roy. Arunava Pal. Ranjan D'Souza. Vikram Mehta.

None had addresses. Only **return information.** The kind you write when you're trying to remember who you are.

He opened one.

If you find this, remember: your name is Neel. You were born in Jalpaiguri. You have a sister who plays the flute. You arrived here in 1972. You are not just a record. You were loved. You laughed. You lived. Please don't forget. Not again.

Rudra read it twice.

He suddenly felt cold.

The air shifted, and he noticed a mirror nailed to the far wall.

Not full-length. Small. Cracked clean through the center.

He walked toward it.

Two reflections stared back at him—**both versions of himself**. One stood straighter, alert, expectant. The other sagged, eyes darker, as if some essential light had gone missing long ago.

Neither blinked when he did.

The next morning, Ananya was gone.

No one saw her leave. No footprints. No farewell. Her room was empty, the cot still warm. The water trough still held the compass, untouched.

Deven Bhatt met him by the well. His face gave nothing away.

"She left," Rudra said.

Deven stirred the fire in the brazier beside him. "No one leaves. Not really."

Rudra clenched his jaw. "Why was she taken?"

"She remembered too quickly."

"What does that mean?"

Deven looked at him, eyes gentler than they had any right to be. "This village holds you until you're ready to forget again. She wasn't. You weren't, either."

Back in his room, Rudra opened his journal.

A new entry had appeared:

She remembers too fast. She had to go.

They always return eventually.

You did.

He stared at the last line.

You did.

The words pulsed on the page, as if they were alive. As if they were **calling something back into his mind**.

He whispered them. Once. Then again.

And suddenly, there was a flash—**a memory**, brief and sharp.

He was standing at a rail platform. A younger version of himself. Holding a sealed envelope, looking up at a station board that read:

KAALGAON – Arrivals Only

Then the image was gone.

That afternoon, he confronted Deven.

"I need to know how long I've been here."

Deven sipped his tea. "Everyone wants to know that."

"Answer me."

The old man tapped the ground with his cane. "We don't keep clocks. We keep pages. Some fade. Some reappear."

"Why me?"

"Because you mapped too much. You trusted borders more than questions."

Rudra was quiet.

Deven added softly, "You stopped remembering what home felt like."

Rudra returned to his room and unrolled the original topographic map—the one from the envelope.

His hands trembled.

Everything was still there—the ridges, the tree lines, the elevation curves. But where **Kaalgaon** should have been, there was only **white space**. Not even a smudge. No settlement. No contour. No name.

Just void.

And in the bottom-right corner, something new had appeared:

A single fingerprint.

Burnt into the paper. Blackened. Deep.

His own.

That night, he dreamed of a railway station again. Not like before.

It was underground, endless, humming. The tracks glowed dimly under his feet. There were no trains—only voices, echoing from every tunnel.

They weren't speaking.

They were **reading**—from journals. His journal. All the ones on the library shelves. Pages being turned. Descriptions being whispered in his own voice.

One phrase repeated across all of them:

You are the map.

He awoke to the sound of footsteps on gravel.

He opened the door and stepped outside.

The fog was thick. The village, as always, half-real in the dusk.

At the edge of the path, by the trees where the trail began, **a man stood**, soaked from head to toe, shivering. A knapsack slung across one shoulder.

Rudra moved closer.

The man looked up.

And Rudra saw himself.

Same face. Same scar above the right brow. Same eyes—but full of terror.

The man held out a folded letter. His lips moved, but no words came out.

Rudra took the letter.

On the front, written in smeared graphite, were four words:

To the next me.

Part 4: The Cartographer's Loop

Rudra didn't open the letter right away.

He sat with it on his lap beneath the bare yellow bulb in his room, the same room he had arrived in—or thought he had. Outside, the fog coiled like breath held too long. The village had gone quiet again, the kind of quiet that felt heavy. Intentional.

The envelope felt warm. Not in temperature, but in weight. As though someone had pressed it against their chest before handing it over. The handwriting was unmistakably his.

He unfolded it.

To the next me,

If you're reading this, then I didn't leave.

Or if I did, I came back.

You are Rudra Thakur. You were born in Sundarnagar. You trained in cartography at the Dehradun Institute. Your first solo field survey was in Bharmour. You broke your wrist in 2016 while tracing ridge lines in the dark. You love aloo paratha with extra ghee.

These are facts. But they won't save you.

You think you arrived here for a survey. You think Kaalgaon is a village you missed on a map. But this place didn't appear on the map by mistake.

It appeared because of you.

He stared at the words for a long time.

The oil lamp flickered.

He looked around the room—his bag, the rolled maps, the journal.

And suddenly, something broke through the haze of his memory. A smell.

Smoke and damp wool. A house burning somewhere distant. His mother screaming. His father trying to unroll a map that kept catching fire.

He saw a **young boy**, staring at a blank sheet of paper, crying because **the lines wouldn't stay in place**.

The next morning, he found Deven standing at the edge of the woods, near the path that curled back toward the trailhead.

"You met yourself," the old man said, not asking.

Rudra nodded.

Deven gestured to the trees. "Do you know why no one ever returns from Kaalgaon with a report?"

"Because they're trapped?"

"No." Deven turned toward him, his eyes clear. "Because the map remembers what the man forgets."

Rudra blinked. "What does that mean?"

Deven pointed toward the hills. "You've been drawing Kaalgaon your whole life. You just didn't know where to place it."

Back in the library, Rudra pulled out a different journal—one he hadn't noticed before. Its label had worn off. The pages inside were filled with overlapping entries, as though **multiple versions of someone had written over each other**.

Each one began with:

"Arrival – Gridpoint R7-32B."

But the names changed.

Karan Thakur. Devraj Singh. Rudra T. Rajan Das. R. Thakur.

All the handwriting was nearly identical. Different strokes. Same voice.

In the middle of the journal, someone had drawn a map.

It showed a loop.

A perfect, enclosed path with no origin point. Just a trail that folded into itself.

At its center, in tiny red ink, someone had written:

"Here lies the surveyor."

That evening, the villagers gathered in the central square.

No one spoke.

There was no fire. Just a single map, pinned to a wooden board. Rudra stepped forward. It was a hand-drawn replica of the region—Himachal's north ridge, with every settlement accounted for. Every forest, trail, and ridge.

Except one.

Kaalgaon was missing.

Only when he tilted his head slightly did he notice it.

There was a faint **thumbprint**, smudged near the lower edge of the R7 grid.

Burned into the paper. His fingerprint.

"Did I die here?" he asked Deven quietly.

"No," the old man replied. "But you dissolved."

Rudra's voice was dry. "And if I go back?"

"You won't make it far. But if you do, the world won't recognize you."

"Why?"

Deven looked at him with something like sorrow. "Because you'll have no coordinates."

That night, Rudra tried something reckless.

He packed his bag. Took the map. Left the journal behind.

And began walking—back along the trail, through the spiraled trees, past the sign that had once read **To Shillak – Or Further**.

He walked until morning.

And found himself standing at the gates of **Kaalgaon.**

Again.

Same mist. Same silence.

The village hadn't changed.

But this time, the villagers **didn't look up** when he passed. No one greeted him. Not even Deven.

He entered his room.

The journal was waiting for him on the table, open to a new page:

You tried.

You walked the loop.

You are closer now.

Later, at sunset, he stood by the well and saw her again.

Ananya.

Only now, her hair was shorter. Her boots newer. Her knapsack different. A slightly younger version of the woman he remembered.

She looked up. Their eyes met.

This time, she smiled.

And in her hand was **his old compass.**

Part 5: The Mapmaker's Memory

Rudra didn't remember writing the new map.

But it was there—unfolded on his desk. Detailed, precise, labeled in his own handwriting.

KAALGAON sat at the center now. Its coordinates freshly inked. Its paths measured, its altitude noted. In the corner, a signature:

Survey Completed: Rudra Thakur

He hadn't signed it.

Not yet.

He returned to the library. His journal now had pages from before his own arrival. One entry was dated five years ago.

It described the same path, the same fog, the same old man.

Same arrival.

But it was signed:

Rudra T. – Archivist, not Surveyor.

He looked up at the mirror.

His reflection was already older. Greyer. A line near his eye that hadn't been there yesterday.

Something had shifted. The houses looked newer. Or older. He couldn't tell anymore. He couldn't tell anymore. Time here didn't flow. It looped. It swirled like smoke inside a bottle.

At dusk, he walked to the well. **Ananya** stood there again.

Only now, she didn't look startled. Her movements were deliberate. Her clothes were cleaner. She didn't carry her bag the way a new arrival did. She held the compass with both hands—*not like a tool, but like a keepsake.*

She turned slowly as he approached.

"Do you remember which direction you came from?" she asked gently.

He stared at her.

That was the same question he'd been told to ask her, when she first arrived.

Only now… she was asking him.

He opened his mouth to answer, but the words caught like paper in fire. His voice felt miles away.

She smiled. The same smile he must have worn the first time around.

That night, he opened his journal.

A new page had written itself:

The village was mapped.

The cartographer was remembered.

Balance has been restored.

He read the lines again and again. He closed the book and ran his fingers across the wooden table, just to feel something real. Something not scripted into the page.

But the table didn't feel like his.

Nothing did anymore.

He looked at the map again. At his signature.

It was dry now. Ink set like stone.

He packed his bag at dawn.

Not out of hope—but necessity.

He walked past the houses, past the broken signpost, back toward the forest. The trail looked the same as when he had first arrived. He paused at the tree line, looked over his shoulder.

Kaalgaon was still there. Waiting.

He stepped into the woods.

For hours, he walked.

He followed the sun, though it never really rose. The sky stayed gray—undecided, like a story unsure of its ending.

Eventually, the trail widened.

He could hear a train.

He emerged onto a platform.

Not Shimla. Not Solan. Not anywhere he remembered.

But the platform was real.

Wooden bench. Dusty tracks. A lamp flickering against a concrete wall.

And on the wall, three painted letters—partially faded:

K—A—A

It was too worn to tell if it once said Kaalgaon.

He waited.

And eventually, a train came.

But Rudra didn't get on.

Instead, he turned around.

The moment his feet touched the first step of the waiting room, he felt it—the weight of his own presence being rewritten.

Inside, there was no station master. No clock. Only a clipboard.

It sat on the desk. Fresh paper. Red ink.

The header said:

Incoming Surveyor – Gridpoint R7-32B

Beneath that, his own name was fading. Like ink left too long in the sun.

He blinked.

And it was gone.

Later that evening, a train stopped at **Kaalgaon Station**. Just long enough for one passenger to step down.

A man.

Tired. Eyes heavy with data and doubt. A bag filled with compasses and surveying tools.

He looked around. Confused.

The station had no signboard.

Only a child, waiting by the gate, holding a clipboard.

"Welcome," the child said. "We've been waiting for you."

The man blinked. "Where is this?"

The child turned the clipboard around.

There was a map on it.

And at the center, in red ink, was a name he didn't recognize:

Kaalgaon

Ten

Scarface

Vikram

You want the truth? Sit down. Don't move. Don't talk. Just listen. Because I'm only gonna tell this once, and you need to hear it straight.

They call me Scarface. Like it's a legend. Like it's something I should be proud of. I didn't ask for the name. Didn't want it. But in this life you don't get to choose. You get the name they give you, and you earn it with blood.

I came up in the tall grass. Couldn't see a damn thing. Couldn't trust anyone. My mother taught me early: stay quiet, keep your ears open, learn to smell the wind before it changes on you. She was tough as bone. Didn't tell bedtime stories. Told us the world was waiting to eat us alive, and you'd better bite first.

My old man? He didn't speak much. He didn't need to. One stare could shut your mouth for days. He ran everything. Decided who ate and who didn't. Where you slept, if you slept at all. He taught us the only lesson that mattered: power isn't given—it's taken. And once you have it, you don't ever let it go.

We watched him. Studied him. That was our mistake. Because you don't stay in the old man's house forever. One day he looks at you and he doesn't see family anymore. He sees threat. That was it. No conversation. No warning. Just snarls, teeth, and blood. Exile.

Four of us made it out. Hunter. Morani. Sikio. Me. Exiles. Nobodies. We weren't a crew yet, just half-starved bastards with enough hate to keep us warm. We learned the rules in the dirt. Learned to steal scraps from the real killers. Waited in the grass for hours to make one clean move. That was our education.

When we were ready? We didn't sneak back in. We hit them at dawn, screaming for blood. We didn't ask. We didn't negotiate. We took. Made sure they knew exactly who we were. Made sure they understood there was no coming back. And yeah—we cleansed the bloodline. Don't look away. That's the rule. You leave them alive? You're raising your replacements.

I remember their mothers. Hating us. Spitting at us. But they didn't leave. Because they needed us. Hate doesn't keep you safe. We did. We set the laws. We enforced them. We made sure everyone ate—even if they ate after us.

We didn't just run it. We built it. Split the territory. No squabbles. No betrayal. We'd sit under the stars at night, laughing, watching for trouble on the horizon. For a while? It worked. It was perfect.

But you know what no one tells you? Power doesn't last.

Time is the real enemy. Hunter got sick. Couldn't keep up. Morani lost a step. Slowed down. Sikio—I'll never forget. Sent him to handle a sit-down. Thought it was business. They butchered him. Left him twitching in the dirt. When I found him, he just stared at me with those empty eyes, asking *How did we let this happen?*

After that it was me. Scarface. The last man standing. They thought the scar meant weakness. That I was beatable. They didn't know it was my badge of survival. Some punk split me open from brow to jaw. Thought he had me. I bled so much the ground drank it. But I didn't fall. I tore his throat out with my teeth and stood up leaking, half-blind, but alive. That's what they remembered. That I'd crawl through my own blood to keep what was mine.

But it got harder. Every year. Food dried up. Rivals multiplied. The next generation didn't give a damn about what we built. They just wanted the throne.

And then came the betrayal.

I took in a young buck. Smart. Fast. Reminded me of me. I trusted him. Fed him. Gave him a slice of the territory. He smiled, nodded, called me boss. Then one night, I turned my back—and he struck. Him and three others. Cut me down in my sleep, dragged me from my home, left me for dead in the ravine.

They thought that was it. They thought the crown was theirs.

I laid there for two days. Couldn't move. Vultures circled. Bones broken. Blood everywhere. I thought it was over.

But something deep inside—something old and angry— kept me breathing.

I remembered what the old man said once, back when I was a kid, crouching behind the brush watching him destroy a rival with a single blow. He said, "If you get knocked down, you get up meaner."

So I did.

It took weeks to heal. I dragged myself through mud, through thorns, through the dark. I watched my kingdom from the shadows. Saw what they did with it. They poisoned it. Fought over scraps. Ruled with panic, not power. They didn't earn it. They inherited it from a body they *thought* was cold.

I came back on a full moon.

They were sleeping. Arrogant. Lazy. Spoiled. I walked into the middle of the territory like a ghost from the old world. No warning. No mercy. Took the first one's throat out before he could scream. The second ran—I let him. The third tried to fight. Poor bastard.

And the kid? The one I trusted? He begged. Said he was wrong. Said he didn't mean it. Said it was the others. I stared him dead in the eye and said, "You should've finished the job."

Then I reminded him what loyalty *used* to mean.

After that, nobody questioned who ruled. Not again.

But it weighs on you. Every year. The hunger. The hate. The ghosts. I see every face I put down. Every brother I buried. Every enemy I flayed open. They don't go away. They watch you. From the grass. From the shadows.

You want me to say sorry? I'm not. You want me to say I'd do it different? Maybe. But this world doesn't let you choose softness. You survive, or you vanish.

Now? I feel the ground under me. Cold. Damp. Breath coming slow. Heavy. I see everything. My mother's eyes. My old man's glare. My brothers laughing. The blood. The betrayals. The victories. The losses.

It's funny. I thought I'd live forever. I thought I was untouchable. Turns out I'm just another body in the dirt, waiting for the light to go out.

But listen to me—don't you dare forget who I was. I took this kingdom with blood in my teeth. I faced down rivals who ran screaming. I killed a hippo one on one with nothing but rage and bone. I made the laws here. I enforced them. And even now, on my last breath, I'll say it clear

Yes. I'm the king of this jungle.

I'm Scarface.

Life Is Too Short

Shivanshi

It all began as a mere bet. It was nothing more than a bet between me and my friends, but who would have thought that actually I would fall in love with her. Looking back, I am not even able to understand what prompted me to fall in love with her. When did it all start?

I guess it was during my high school years. I had to move to New York because of my mother's business, leaving my brother and father in Italy. It was my new school life starting and I was pretty excited.

Everyone spoke freely and socialised with me. I never really felt alone with everyone around. I joined the basketball club and continued my passion. I hung around with my friends and we always played games and had a good time together. 2 years passed in a blink. It was on one Sunday evening when we were at my place hanging out. We were so bored that we began playing Truth or Dare.

I used to believe love was something that happened in slow motion—like in the movies. A lingering glance, a dramatic confession, maybe a kiss in the rain. I never thought mine would begin with a bet. A dare, of all things.

It was stupid. A harmless game during a late-night hangout with the basketball team. Sam had dared me during Truth or Dare to do something "fun" with a twist.

"Alright, Ethan," he grinned, spinning a bottle between us.

"We all know you're the charmer here. Let's see if you can get the quietest girl in the entire school to talk to you."

"The quietest girl?" I blinked. Sam and Luke looked at each other and smirked at each other.

"Yeah," chimed Luke, laughing. "That Natalie chick. You know—the one with the books, specs and hoodies? Barely even speaks."

"Let's spice it up," Luke added with a devilish grin. "You get her to smile, we owe you pizza for a week. You get her to fall for you—Ethan, we'll worship you."

It was meant to be a joke. I accepted with a shrug and a laugh.

"Bet," I said.

One word. That one word would come back to haunt me more deeply than I'd ever imagined.

Natalie, that name lingered and curiosity built up as I have never seen her. Then I met her in the gymnasium. I didn't even know her name back then. She walked in like she didn't belong, eyes scanning the place nervously. Her presence was quiet, like a whisper in a storm—but something about her made me stop.

She wasn't like the others. She wasn't trying to be noticed. She wasn't bending herself into a mold just to fit in. She stood there, awkward, unsure, and real. I'd never seen anyone like her. She was quite the opposite of everyone I saw thus far.

Her eyes scanned around trying to find someone.

"Ethan, focus here…" Sam tossed the basketball at full throttle towards me. I moved on reflex and the ball headed towards her. My heart practically froze.

"CAREFUL!" I yelled and ran to her. I pulled her away just in time. We crashed to the floor with force. She grunted. I was about to speak, to apologise and ask if she was ok –

"NATALIE! Don't break Ethan's bones!" yelled a girl crouching next to me. Everyone snickered hearing her comment. That was pretty mean. I was about to retaliate but she, who was quiet, sat up and glared.

"Natalie, what are you even doing in a gymnasium?" scoffed the girl reaching her hand to help me. Normally I would feel quite glad for the help yet this time it kind of infuriated me. I refused her help and stood up.

"What is your statement supposed to mean?" she asked, raising an eyebrow from irritation. The girls began snickering and few even broke into hyena laughter. "Come on Nat, we all know you are not suited for sports or gym." She snickered and smirked.

Natalie huh… That's who she is. I looked at her and she was visibly irritated. Veins bulged on her forehead. She bit her lower lip, "Hannah Peterson, Mrs. Ivy has called for you. Get going! Please let Mrs. Ivy know that I will be back in about 30 minutes." She announced making it reach her friend in a corner. Her friend nodded and quickly.

Natalie's eyes then fell on the girl who began picking on her who declared her unwanted in the gymnasium. "If you must know, I am a throw ball player at National Level who led our country a year back leading us to win the previous cup and also a badminton and basketball player at State level."

The entire gymnasium froze to silence. A stunned silence.

Her mouth gaped wide in shock. "Don't be delusional. You only led them. You didn't play well at all!" she yelled.

I must say, Natalie piqued my curiosity. Natalie's eyes scrutinized the other girl. "Seeing your jersey makes me realize you are a throw ball player aren't you?" Natalie asked, crossing her arms and looking straight into the girl's eyes. "Why don't we do a one versus nine match?"

"Yo bro! What are you looking at?" Sam threw an arm around my neck.

"Looking at an interesting match…"

"Oh, Nat's in business huh?"

"You know her?"

"Come on bro, Natalie is in my class and she is a good basketball and throw ball player. But she refuses to play because of some reason…" he announced beside me and reduced his voice barely above a whisper, "Plus she is your dare…"

Only one word rang in my mind. 'INTERESTING'

My focus fell on them again. Natalie stood tall and unaffected where the other girl took a fatal blow in her pride.

"You dare our team? Alright you are on!"

One might think that she was being haughty or impulsive acting as she pleased, but you should never let those who trample you slide by, right?

They then proceeded to the court. Those girls began planning as a team. Natalie on the other hand removed her specs and changed into her contacts and tied her long hair into a bun. The match began, and the air in the gymnasium shifted. Everyone's attention was now focused on the impromptu game, curiosity piqued by the confrontation. My entire focus fell on Natalie and her bold attitude. She took a deep breath, as if it was meant to calm a calamity within her.

The referee blew the whistle, and the game started.

The opposing team served first, and their captain smirked, aiming for what she assumed was their plus point. But as if Natalie had anticipated her move, with a swift, calculated step to the left, she caught the ball effortlessly, redirecting it across the net with a sharp, precise throw. It struck the ground in their court before any of them could react.

"One-zero," the referee called out, and I could see their smug expressions falter at her counter.

The game continued, and her every move was fluid, precise, and controlled. She darted across the court with speed and agility that left the audience in awe. The ball became an extension of her, moving wherever she willed it to go. She used their overconfidence to her advantage, luring them into making hasty decisions and then exploiting their mistakes.

The opposing team tried to rally, but their coordination faltered under her unrelenting attacks. They aimed to overwhelm her with their numbers, but she countered with skill, anticipating their every move. Her throws were fast and strategic, targeting the weak spots in their formation. Her defense was solid; not a single ball touched her side of the court without a fight.

By the middle of the game, she had gained a significant lead. The crowd, which initially seemed indifferent, now cheered louder with each point she scored. Damn she is good…

"Seven-zero," the referee announced.

The opposing team grew desperate, their movements frantic and disorganized. Their captain yelled instructions, but the pressure was too much.

When the score reached nine-zero, the gym was silent except for the sound of her footsteps and the ball hitting the ground. The final serve was hers. She took a deep breath, locked eyes with the opposing captain, and launched the ball with all her strength. It sailed over the net with incredible speed, striking the far corner of their court. None of them even moved.

"Ten-zero," the referee called, signaling the end of the game.

The gym erupted into applause. She straightened up, wiping the sweat off her brow, and removed her contact and switched to glasses, adjusting them with calm composure.

I stood at the edge of the court, my eyes glued to her. My brothers nearby whispered something but none of that went inside my ears. It was as if my whole soul was attracted to her. She noticed me looking at her. She did a polite bow and mouthed thank you. She crouched down, re-tying her laces. I approached her, offering my hand to help her up from her crouched position.

"That was incredible" I said, my voice filled with genuine awe.

She smiled, a small, confident one. Her eyes flicked to the bully. "Don't ever underestimate someone based on appearances" she said, meeting her gaze. "You might just be surprised."

With that she walked off. I ran behind her. Something told me, if I don't strike up a conversation now, it's never. I walked fast with long strides and caught up to her.

"Wait up Natalie!"

"What is it?" She asked, her eyes squinting.

"I just wanted to say, that was seriously impressive. I don't think I've ever seen anyone take down a whole team like that."

"Thanks... I have had my share of practice"

"Practice? You mean dominating opponents and leaving everyone speechless?"

Her lips pressed and curved into a smile, "Perhaps something on that line."

Over the next few days I shadowed her. I started showing up wherever she was. Library? I was suddenly very interested in ancient history. Cafeteria? I just happened to change tables. Hallway? I 'coincidentally' took longer routes to class. At first, it was for the dare... then it became something else.

I wanted to know her.

One afternoon, she was in the library, immersed in a book. I sat across from her at the table. Looking up, her eyes looked so big and beautiful. She tilted her head showcasing her confusion.

"Do you always read such heavy stuff?" I asked, tilting my head to read the title of her book.

"I like it, why are you here? Don't you have practice or something?"

I shrugged. "I do, but I figured I'd take a break and learn a bit about the mysterious girl who wiped the floor with nine players at once."

She raised an eyebrow. "Mysterious?"

"Well, you don't exactly share much," I pointed out. "I'm Ethan, by the way. In case you forgot."

She rolled her eyes. "I know who you are. The entire school knows who you are."

"And now, I know who you are, Natalie, the throw ball champ."

"What do you want, Ethan?" Her voice sharp and perhaps a bit guarding.

"Just to talk, and maybe to figure out how you managed to be so incredible without anyone noticing, bellezza."[Bellezza meaning beauty]

"You speak Italian?" her voice rang with surprise.

"Of course, as someone from Italy, I do." I chuckled. My eyes locked against her. "How do you know it's Italian, bambina?"[Bambina meaning baby or baby-girl]

"Oh well, during elementary our school brought in extra subjects where students must learn a new language. I chose Italian because I thought it was a cool place when I was young…" she said, staring at my book.

"Do you think it isn't a cool place now?" I asked with a small smirk on my lips. She shook her head negatively.

She then chuckled and said, "Piacere, Ethan"[Piacere meaning nice to meet you]

"Piacere, Natalie!" I smiled back. We chatted quietly in Italian, giggling and smiling to our hearts' content.

Days skipped by, perhaps merrily? Every day was new, a new opportunity to talk with Natalie. But as if guilt was plaguing my heart, I felt like I ought to apologize to her. Is it because I didn't stand up for her when she was bullied or because I reached out to her only for a dare? That evening I jogged up to her.

"Hey, Nat!"

She stopped, frowning. "Are you stalking me now?"

"Maybe" I joked, then quickly added, "Okay, no. I just wanted to apologize."

"For what?"

"For what happened in the gym. The way those girls treated you. I should've said something."

She was taken aback. "You didn't have to. I handled it. Plus its way back, don't sweat it!"

"I know," I said, softening my voice. "But it wasn't right. And I wanted you to know that I think you're amazing. Not just because of what you did, but because you stood up for yourself."

She blinked in disbelief and then chuckled. "Apology accepted!"

My persistence paid off. The invisible wall around her melted away with each day of our interactions. We began talking more. I would sit with her during breaks, walk her to class, and even join her in the library, pretending to study while asking her endless questions about her life.

Through these small gestures, Natalie became a constant in my life, someone who didn't just see me as the "hot jock to hang-out with" but as someone worth knowing.

And though she was reluctant at first, she relaxed over time. For the first time, I felt like maybe, just maybe, I can make it all work.

It was after another casual evening at the library, where I'd sat across from her pretending to read while sneaking glances her way. Her eyes constantly kept glancing up and looking at me quietly.

"Ethan" she said, closing her book, her eyes locking at me.

"Yeah?" I leaned forward, my usual playful grin on my face.

"What are we?" Her voice was steady.

I blinked, caught off guard. "What do you mean?"

"I mean… us. You've been spending so much time with me. Are we just friends, or…?" She swallowed without saying another word.

Without much warning, my grin was replaced with a soft smile. "I thought it was obvious, Nat. I like you. A lot."

"You like me?" Her eyes widened and fiddled her fingers.

"Ti Amo" I said, standing and moving closer. "Natalie, will you be my girlfriend?"[Ti amo meaning I love you]

She didn't speak for some time. After a few seconds which felt like eternity, her eyes brimmed with tears. Her hands tightened and she nodded, "Yes, Ethan!"

My smile widened, and I pulled her into a gentle hug. I gently pecked her cheek and I gleamed like a child who got a bag full of candy. I walked her home despite its distance and before I left, "Sei bello, Nat! Boun Notte…" I pecked her cheek and started walking then I stopped and turned to her, "Ti amo, Terso"[Sei Bello meaning you are beautiful and Boun Notte meaning Good Night]

That night I was sleepless. I looked at the ceiling completely dazed. I turned and toiled in the bed until my throat felt parched. I decided to get myself a glass of water. I stopped in my tracks when I heard my mother's voice.

The lights in the living room were on. "Do you think he got a new friend?" My dad's voice resounded loud in the silent room over the phone.

"Friend? Darling he is love struck" my mom giggled as she spoke. "Even though I may not agree to him dating some random girl"

"A girl? With this dummy? No way!" My father yelled.

"Keep it down darling. If he is happy, then he is. It has been a long time since he felt comfortable after coming from Italy"

I didn't interrupt them and went back to my room. This time the moment my head hit the bed I fell asleep hoping that this happiness doesn't shatter like a dream.

Days felt blissful. Whenever she came out or was in the corridor I was there. I accompanied her everywhere and everyone knew about us being a thing. I even introduced her to my friends and she also came to cheer me on during my games.

During our small meets we played basketball together, conversed in Italian and it was lovely. I am glad that I confessed to her. Our relationship wasn't anything fancy. It was heartwarming enough to keep us both happy… or so I thought….

The graduation party was a milestone. I took Natalie as my date. She opposed me from picking her up and said she will come to surprise me. The room was alive with laughter and music, filled with glittering lights and beautifully dressed students.

My heart raced, when I saw Nat walk in with her beautiful blue prom frock, she was charming and elegant effortlessly. I waved at her and she smiled. She was busy herself. My eyes fell on her occasionally.

My guys and I decided to go to the balcony for some air. The air was cool and soothing. But who would have thought that this cool night would be a disaster for life.

"Dude, I still can't believe you got her to fall for you," Sam said, his voice loud and mocking. "I mean, Natalie? Of all people?"

I froze.

"Yeah," Luke chimed in. "You've got to admit, it's impressive. The shy girl who wouldn't talk to anyone— now she's head over heels for you. It's almost cute."

I sighed, sounding annoyed. "Come on, guys. Don't talk about her like that."

"Relax, man," Luke said. "It's just funny how she's so clueless about how things started."

"What's that supposed to mean?" I asked, my tone sharp.

"You know. The whole bet thing," Sam replied.

"It wasn't like that. I didn't—" I began.

"You didn't have to. We all saw how hard you worked to get her attention," Luke said with a laugh. The laughter froze with a loud shattering. My blood ran cold when I saw Nat stand in the entrance tearing running down her cheeks. She trembled.

"Nat…" I stepped forward.

"Don't…" she said, stepping back.

"Wait, let me explain,"

"Explain what, Ethan?" She said, her voice trembling. "Explain how I was just some kind of joke to you? A game for you and your friends to laugh about?"

"It wasn't like that"

"Don't lie to me!" Her voice cracked. The room felt suffocating, the weight of her words crushing my chest.

"I trusted you, Ethan, I believed in you. I thought… I thought you cared about me."

"I do care about you" I said, my voice breaking.

"If you cared, you wouldn't have let this happen. You wouldn't have continued your game if you truly knew how tough it had been for me. Couldn't you find anything better to toy with other than my feelings? Other than my heart and my love? Was I truly nothing more than a bet?" The silence between us was deafening. My friends stood awkwardly, their laughter now replaced by guilt-ridden stares.

"TI ODIO Ethan!"[Ti odio meaning I hate you]

She ran out. I ran behind her but she disappeared in thin air. My fear became a reality. She got hurt because of me. What a jerk I am! I was in no mood to continue the party. I left abruptly and went home only to find my dad and brother here to visit us.

"Where is your girl?" My mom asked, setting down plates for dinner, as I told her about Natalie before departing to the party.

"I… Well… We had a fight…"

"Good gracious! That poor girl…" my brother began but I didn't pay any attention to them. I went to my room. Every single word from her felt like a blow to my heart.

You are stupid Ethan! You betrayed a good girl! I lost the girl I loved because of my foolishness!

Days skipped by quickly. Timetable for the final examinations came by. I checked my timetable and Nat's timetable. Her exams starts a week later after mine.

Soon a week passed by. I completed my exams and waited for Natalie to come. She had her head down on her novel with her headset on. I stood in front of her and she lifted her head up.

I could find everyone around us whispering and they were kind of cheering on. Well then again, except me, her and my friends, no one knows about what happened that day. She faked a smile "I am busy. I need to study, so rest up" and walked past me without a word.

This continued for a week. I always stood outside when she came out after completing her exam and I never uttered a word or rather she never let me to.

Finally exams were done! She came out and there I was again. She was about to walk past me but this time I removed her headset and held it high. "Shall we talk?" I asked, looking serious.

"Sure"

I grabbed her hand tight and strode fast across the corridors. Finally we reached the gymnasium and I stopped once we were inside the gym. I let go of her hand and she was about to speak when I pinned her to the wall and punched the wall hard.

"What has gotten into you!" she yelled, looking at my knuckles bleeding out.

"Will you please listen to my explanation?" I begged, my eyes close to tears.

She nodded.

"Natalie, I am so sorry that I hurt you. I shouldn't have agreed on the stupid bet. It is true, I came talking to you for the bet. But that completely changed when I started to talk to you." I kept gazing at her constantly. She looked at me silently.

"I confess I wasn't honest in the beginning but once I got to know you more, I couldn't help but fall for you all over again." I gently caressed her cheeks and put my head on her shoulder. "I know I was a jerk. I made you cry on a great day…I was a big jerk….Tell me, what should I do to make you feel less hatred and anger towards me?"

"I don't know what to do either." She paused and looked at me. "Ethan. Alright. Let's do this." She took a deep breath and I lifted my head, looking at her.

"If you truly love me, then come back here to the same gymnasium in 10 years. 7th May 2035, by 6pm. Can you wait that long?"

I looked at her baffled. "If I wait for you, will you accept my apology and…"I bit my lip and stopped, scared she would run away.

"I will. But I am not sure if I can get slim and get pretty…"

"I don't care, you are beautiful both inside and out. Then remember your words." I stepped even closer and leaned in. I pulled her specs off her face and caressed her cheeks gently. I tucked the strand of hair lingering near her forehead behind her ears. Before she could do something, I kissed gently on her lips. She froze.

She pressured her hands against my chest, but I persistently held her in my arms, tightly secured and wrapped around. When I moved away, her lips were practically swollen. "Humor our deal, Natalie. Arrivederci" With that I left her there[Arrivederci meaning goodbye]

When I came back home, my heart was racing. I kissed her! What was I thinking! That…That was our first kiss.

Ten Years Later…

You never know where life takes you. It is a journey that you take on, you don't know where your destination is, and you don't know where are the stops you need to look out for. Pretty mysterious and tiring, isn't it?

Ten years. I spent ten years gathering up the courage to face Natalie a second time. Not because I was worried about being rejected—I probably deserve it—but because I knew I broke something precious. And now I was finally going to attempt to fix it.

I had just returned from a series of consecutive games. My team's winning streak was certainly a big part of the headline news, but this was nothing compared to the jitters twisting in my gut right now. This wasn't a championship game—this was Natalie. The girl I never stopped loving.

I left practice early today, told my coach I had somewhere important to be. He rolled his eyes, but let me leave. If only he knew...this wasn't just important, this was 10 years in the making...

I had rehearsed this a thousand times in my head. I had a feeling that she might show today, but I couldn't be too sure. I didn't want to get my hopes up too much, but Natalie had always kept her promises. I just didn't know if I still had a place in her memories...or her heart.

The gymnasium looked fantastic—our friends did a great job. I contacted the school's administration, reserved the gymnasium, ordered flowers, lights, music—everything she loved. Even managed to sneak in a rose garden renovation. She always loved roses. I was keeping track of every favor I could. Flowers, lights, a garden setup, and even a switch with her name on it. She used to say that she loved surprises, how she loved fairy tales. Well, I was going to try my best to be her fairy tale—eventually.

Then came the hardest part—her family.

Sure, calling her parents was easy. They were civil, maybe even warm. But her brother? Nathan? That was a storm I was willingly walking into. The moment I arrived and he saw me in front of his house, he punched me on the face.

To be honest, I needed it. Then he stared at me like a hawk, but he did help me organize the surprise. Somewhere in there, I think he always wanted Nat to be happy—even if it meant taking the leap to trust me again.

Her parents, even more, surprisingly came around fast. Maybe they saw something in my eyes. Maybe they never hated me, just hated what I'd done. I definitely wasn't the boy I had been 10 years ago—I was a man. A man who knew what he wanted.

And I love Natalie.

I sat in the gym, my heart racing against my chest, and the lights were out. As soon as she opened the door, everything came into focus.

The crowd parted. I walked forward with a bouquet of red roses. She looked stunned. Beautiful, as always— but stunned. She still had the same deep, contemplative eyes, and I forgot to breathe for a moment.

I smirked and tried to slow my heart. "It took you ten years to shine as bright as you always do but with confidence."

She looked back at me and her focus went to the bruise on my face. "What the hell happened to your face?"

I laughed, not picturing this would be the first question she asked. "We meet after 10 years and you want to ask me about this, bambina?"

She still had the same effect on me—totally unpredictable and completely disarming.

I took a deep breath and stepped back, still holding the bouquet tightly. "It took me 10 years to find this courage. Will you accept my apology?"

She smiled. "Okay, I will."

I swear my heart burst at that moment.

I wasn't finished yet.

I dropped down to one knee, pulled out the ring box and pushed it towards her. "Will you marry me, Nat?"

The squeals from our old classmates behind me did not matter. At that moment, in the universe, it was just Natalie and I. Her expression softened, and I acknowledged that her mind was going a mile a minute.

"Who did you bet with?" she asked suspiciously.

I laughed, caught red handed, "No one...well yeah I did bet with one."

Her eyes widened.

"I bet myself to love you more."

She made that face; the one that said you lucky I love you, then smiled.

"You better!"

As I slid the ring onto her finger and pulled her in for a hug, the world melted away. I kissed her forehead and incredibly enjoyed the feeling of her warmth again.

"Don't make her cry!" a loud voice shouted.

Natalie stiffened and looked in the direction of the voice. "Dad? Mom? What are you guys doing here?"

"Don't forget about me, sister!" Nathan grinned.

I looked at her sheepishly. "I'm going to need their blessing if I want to marry you."

"You can always kick him if he turns out to be a jerk, bambina," Mother said.

"Mother, that is not how you support your son!" I groaned.

Nathan leaned in and whispered something in Natalie's ear. She was shocked, "You punched him?" could be heard across the gym.

"Of course you should, Nathan!" Dad said proudly. "This Son of mine, for crying out loud, is dumb as a stump anyways."

Laughter, teasing, joy. This was what I wanted. What I fought for. I walked over wrapping my hands around her waist, "Darling, I will make sure you will not regret choosing me"

Her blue eyes shone like sapphire. "I trust you, Ethan" She leaned on my arm and stood quietly enjoying the moment. This very moment felt like a dream. I was scared that I might wake up to find this happiness gone like a wistful dream. If this is a dream, let me keep dreaming.

Life is too short for worrying. Be happy! That is all that matters at the end of the day!

Twelve

The Colors of Love

Madhavan

1. The Train of Strangers

The train from Delhi to Varanasi was packed, as always. It was an overnight journey, and the air buzzed with murmurs in many languages — Hindi, English, Bengali, Tamil, and even a bit of Arabic.

In one compartment, six strangers sat across from each other — their eyes occasionally meeting, then darting away.

None of them knew that over the next 24 hours, they would discover something deeper than the journey itself.

They would discover love — not the romantic kind alone, but the kind that transcends cultures and hearts.

2. Meet the Travelers

Ayesha, 24, from Hyderabad, wearing a hijab and carrying a small Urdu poetry book. She was on her way to

Varanasi for a research paper on Sufi influence in Hindu sacred cities.

Kabir, 28, from Punjab, with a turban and a camera around his neck. He was a wedding photographer returning from a shoot.

Mei Lin, 30, from China, dressed in a simple cotton kurta, learning Hindi and traveling across India for spiritual reasons. She clutched a worn-out diary.

Eli, 35, from Israel, with a backpack full of sketchpads. He painted faces of people he met and believed in documenting emotions.

Thatha, 72, from Chennai, a retired Tamil professor visiting Kashi for what he called his "final pilgrimage."

And a boy named Anshu, barely 11, traveling alone, holding a red rose wrapped in tissue paper.

Their journeys were separate.

But love would bind them.

3. The Conversation Begins

As the train clattered on, a silence lingered — until the boy, Anshu, asked loudly:

"Can I ask something?"

The others looked at him, amused.

"Go ahead," said Kabir with a grin.

"Is it okay for boys to give flowers to boys?"

The group paused. Mei Lin smiled gently. Ayesha looked up from her book. Even Thatha leaned in.

"Why do you ask?" Eli inquired.

Anshu hesitated, then said, "My best friend is moving away. He always protected me. I wanted to give him this rose tomorrow. But my uncle said it's not right... that love like that is shameful."

The rose trembled in his tiny hand.

The strangers looked at each other — the kind of look that needs no words.

Thatha spoke first.

"In Tamil, we have a word — 'Anbu'. It means love. Not romantic, not family. Just... love. It is sacred. It needs no permission."

Ayesha added softly, "In Sufism, we say 'Ishq' is the purest form of love — it flows between friends, strangers, between the soul and God."

Mei Lin nodded. "In Chinese culture, giving flowers is a deep gesture. It shows gratitude, not just romance. I gave one to my teacher when I left home."

Kabir leaned in. "In Punjab, boys hug, cry, dance — all in love. It's not about gender. It's about heart."

Anshu looked at them — six strangers, each so different, yet all saying the same thing.

Eli, the Israeli painter, reached for his sketchpad.

"Come here, I want to draw you holding that rose. One day, you'll see what courage looks like."

4. The Heart Opens

As night deepened, so did the stories.

Ayesha spoke of her late grandfather who used to recite Urdu poetry to her grandmother every morning, even when Alzheimer's stole her memory.

"He said, even if she forgets me, I will remind her with love."

Kabir shared how his sister married a man from Kerala. At first, the family objected — different language, food, customs. But love won. Today, their Punjabi-Malayali home is a mix of dosas and butter chicken.

Mei Lin told them she left her job as a banker in Beijing after a heartbreak. She came to India to learn how to heal — not through medicine, but through connection.

"I learned the word 'seva' here — selfless service. In that, I found love again."

Eli pulled out a sketch of a widow he had met in Pushkar.

"She lit a diya for her late husband every evening — not because she missed him, but because she loved the peace he brought her."

Thatha, in his old, cracked voice, whispered:

"I was in love once. With a boy in college. In the 1960s. We wrote letters, never posted them. Society would have killed us. I buried that love... but never its memory."

Even the wind outside seemed to pause for his pain.

Ayesha gently held his hand. "You didn't bury love, Thatha. You preserved it."

5. At Midnight: The Festival of Lights

Around midnight, the train passed through a village celebrating an early Diwali. Crackers popped. Diyas lit up the horizon. Children ran alongside the train.

Anshu gasped. "It's so beautiful!"

Mei Lin said, "In China, we light red lanterns to guide spirits. In India, you light lamps to welcome joy."

Thatha smiled. "Light is the same everywhere, child. Only the language changes."

Eli suddenly stood up.

"I want everyone to write what love means to them — one sentence. I'll make a mural with it someday."

They all agreed.

On scraps of paper, in different scripts, they wrote:

- Ayesha: "Love is remembering someone in every prayer."

- Kabir: "Love is when she sees my flaws and still chooses me every morning."

- Mei Lin: "Love is the silence between two people that feels safe."

- Eli: "Love is the emotion I chase with my brush."

- Thatha: "Love is what I lived, even if in secret."

- Anshu: "Love is giving a flower, even if you're scared."

The train rolled on. But something had shifted.

They weren't strangers anymore.

6. Morning Light and Goodbye

At sunrise, the train neared Varanasi Junction.

The ghats appeared in the distance — glowing golden, smoke rising from sacred fires, priests chanting shlokas.

One by one, the travelers prepared to get off.

Thatha, with help from Kabir, stepped down, touching the platform with reverence. "Now I'm ready," he whispered, "to meet the Ganga with a full heart."

Ayesha smiled at Mei Lin. "Thank you for teaching me that courage looks different in every culture."

Mei Lin bowed slightly. "And thank you for showing me that faith can be soft, yet strong."

Kabir gave Anshu a tight hug. "Go give that flower. Tell him why. Even if he doesn't understand now, he will one day."

Eli handed each of them a sketch — small portraits, raw and beautiful. "You're all love stories," he said, "I just drew the truth."

Anshu looked back at them as the train emptied.

"I thought I was alone. But maybe... love is bigger than I knew."

7. Epilogue: Years Later

Years passed.

- Anshu grew up to be a counselor for LGBTQ+ youth in India. In his office was a framed sketch of a boy holding a rose.

- Ayesha became a professor of comparative religion. Her lectures often began with the story of the train and ended with a line: "Love lives in the unlikeliest of journeys."

- Kabir opened a photo studio titled "Rang-e-Mohabbat" — The Colors of Love. He hung photos of intercultural weddings, each telling its own love story.

- Mei Lin returned to China and published a memoir: "Namaste to My Heart", blending Indian philosophy with Eastern poetry.

- Eli's mural, made from the train passengers' words, now hangs in a museum in Jerusalem. At the center, it says in bold:

"LOVE IS UNIVERSAL. CULTURES CHANGE. HEARTS DON'T."

- Thatha's story inspired a play called "The Unposted Letters." It premiered in Chennai and later in Mumbai during Pride Month.

And the train?

Still runs.

Still carries strangers.

Still tells stories.

Thirteen

Amar's Chitra Katha

Divyalakshmi G

Thunder rumbled with a spark of lightning; a thud sound was heard in a lone night road. Amar jumped from the walls of his house. With a fearful gaze, he adjusts his shoulder bag and runs. A 28-year-old, Amar, lean guy with sharp jawline and thick beard had finally gained courage to flee from his house and rushes to the railway station. He boards on a random train waiting at the station, hurries and sits in a window seat. The train starts to move, marking his start of the journey. The sharp choo sound of train was hitting the silent night and Amar lifts up his mobile phone from his jean pocket and turns on the airplane mode, and slowly lays down on his bag, looking at the trees moving past him, he closes his big brown eyes to go to sleep. He suddenly wakes up to the fusty smell, rubs off his nose and holds his chest to control his puke. He looks at the person sitting in front of him, smiling and juice of paan, that he had been chewing is dripping along his mouth. Amar ghastly looks at him and takes up his shoulder bag and moves towards the door of the train. Glowing rays of the sun caresses his face, while he gets ready to depart from the train.

He gets down at the railway station and turns off airplane mode and calls his friend Ravi. "Hey Ravi! I have reached Pather station, when are you coming to pick me up?"

"I can't come man, a fire accident happened at my factory and I'm struggling all things around here. I have arranged a house and cook for you. Just take a bullock cart and go two miles, you will reach the village" Ravi replied

Amar gets tensed and replies "Ravi! Bullock cart ah? I can't go in that dirty cart, arrange me some other vehicle "

Ravi replies "In this village, you can go only by this way, or else walk two miles. Only here your father can't find you. Now cut the call and let me do my work!" and hangs up the call.

Amar bangs his leg on the floor in frustration, decides to walk to the village. He comes out of the station, the earthy smell in the air, people dressed in old aged dhothis and sarees, looked at him differently because of his posh attire. He then adjusts his bag and looks up to walk, while his hand is held by an old man, who has skin wounds all over his body after lifting loads of cotton sack in the scorching sun. Amar looks at his wounds and screams in disgust, immediately pushes and averts, lifts both his hands up in the air and says "dirty old man! Don't touch me!". The old man, falls on the road, struggles to stand up without support, meanwhile Amar walks fast as if nothing had happened. We meet people like Amar in nook and corner of the world who are disgusted by old age and sickness, expect everyone to be dressed neat and well, respect people based on their financial status, but the reality is, not everyone gets everything. Many suffer, struggle, survive, that's the rule of their life. Amar is moneyed and coddled, but wouldn't it be great if people like Amar change themselves and change the society they live in.

Finally, he reaches the village after a painful walk, holds his knees and breathes heavily. A young girl draped in black and red half saree, brown tinted face with a calm smile comes near him and gives him a glass of water. Amar pulls it from her and gulps it in a go. He doesn't even thank her, but rather asks for details on the place, his friend had mentioned. She waves her hand to follow her. She takes him to a tiled roof house, with bright blue paint, rangoli in front of the home, flower plants near the gate of the house. Amar looks astonished and looks at her and starts shouting at her. She looks at him with shrunken eyes and signs "*I'm deaf and dumb, this is only big house in the whole village, Ravi sir told me to keep things clean for you, I don't understand what you are saying, will bring food in a while, looks like you are hungry" and* leaves the house. He tries to clap and call her, but nothing works. Amar drops his bag on the cane knitted sofa and bites his teeth in frustration. Echoing voices of "you need to respect everybody, until then you will learn to grow in life, apologize or get out now!!" was ringing in his ears, he suddenly awakens and wipes of his face and goes for a bath. Amar was yet again shocked by looking at the bathroom, though clean, but toilet and bathing place are together. His whole body shuddered in disgust, fills up, the bucket by opening the tap while holding his nose closed with other. Experience teaches us the value of life and what we cherish in life. Once you step out of the comfort zone, reality hits hard. Amar is now facing the real world, where getting accustomed to new things is an art, once mastered, one can see beauty even in little things. Dresses up neat and Amar switches on the fan, it starts with a "Tak Tak" sound, wherein he immediately puts his hand over head in fear of fan falling, but then realize that it's running fine but with a jarring sound. He hears a knock at the door, a tray with food, water and tea, it was her. He didn't even bother to move the door for her to enter. She smiled and placed everything on the table and signed at him *"I have written my number here, if you need tea, call once, if you need food, call twice"*. Amar nods and turns his head. She leaves the place. Amar is multilingual and had also learned sigh language during his NGO work that his father had pressured him to join. Amar's dad is a self-made richest man, but he always insists on little things in life and values every human. Amar grew up to be a direct opposite to his dad, he was his mother's spoilt brat. Amar took up the tray of food, and gobbled up as if there's no tomorrow. He felt contented after the meal. She came to take up the plates which was scattered around and she cleaned up the mess, he had done while eating. Amar sits on sofa not bothered. She signs *"How was the food?"* Amar be like "yeah it was ok" and stretches his legs in the coffee table. "Ah, give me the purple tea in the evening that you gave with the food". She reads lips with shrunken eye, nods and leaves. After a sound sleep, sips the tea that she had kept in the table and he thinks to go for a stroll. He starts walking, and notice neighbouring hutch house and she was standing at the side and feeding the hens. She looks at him and waves, he smiles and asks "Is this your house? Do you stay alone?". She signs "*Yes sir! I live with my father. Please come inside sir*". Amar forestalled, and says "Ah it's ok, I will come some other day" and tries to leave the place, but looks at a complete white bearded old man, wearing white dhothi and black shirt, comes out of the hutch, stands near the gate and pees on his dhothi. Amar looks at this and shouts at him "Hey oldie! Can't you pee in the bathroom? Are you out of your mind?", While she comes running towards the old man, and takes him to tap and washes him off, Amar is horrified by all these and says "Do you cook for me with same hands; you wash his pee?", looks at him in fury, takes up a fresh dhothi hanging in the washing line and takes her father inside the house. She comes and washes her hand with soap and signs at him "*We maybe poor, but we do know basic cleanliness. My father has dissociative dementia, he barely remembers who he is or what he should do, so sometimes such things happen. You need not worry about this sir!*" Amar raises his shoulders, smirks and leaves to his house. Days and days go on, he keeps ignoring all the texts and calls from his parents. The biggest punishment that we could give to our loved ones is the silent treatment. Loneliness starts to kill him inside, his eyes burst in tears, the silent screams, eventually darkness fills up his life, he starts to miss his mother's caress, father's love but his ego builds up as a wall pushing him underneath. One fine day, he wakes up early and watches the sun rise over the hutch of her house, the glowing sun rays filled up the sky in the golden hour. She comes out of the house carrying strings and toys in her hand, and looks at her washing her hands with soap and prepare tea in an earthenware in the firewood. Suddenly he receives a call from Ravi. Amar picks and says "Finally! You took these many days to call! So, busy huh? Ravi replies "You know my situation Amar, I had to take care of my business! Anyways how's the place? I hope she takes care of you well!" "Tch! Yeah, she gives food on time. But she and her dad! Her dad behaves like a child! Can't she put him on an adult diaper or something! He keeps peeing in front of the house! Oof!! These dirty people, please come soon and help me move from here!" replies aggravatedly."

Ravi replies "Hey! Do you know something? That isn't her own father, he adopted her while she was 5. His own son and daughter abandoned him since he was diagnosed with dementia. He is my father's friend. My father visits him every month, he was a very educated person with good wealth, poor guy, after his wife's death his children took all his money and left him and her. She started to take care of him at her early teen, she sacrificed a lot for him, works multiple jobs to take care of him. Though being deaf and dumb, she is stubborn and persistent to take good care of him. I have never seen her do anything for her. Amar was so shocked to hear this "Hey Ravi, I never knew about this. I think I shouldn't jump to judgements!" replied Amar Ravi then replies "It would be great if you develop empathy and first understand your father!" and hangs up. Amar keeps his phone on the table and dresses up. He opens the door and looks at the hutch house. He then walks to her home, she was standing near the iron spike fence, he slowly approaches near her, she remains undisturbed looking a far, at a newly married couple happily coming from the temple. She wanted to live a normal life, but fate hit her with a bulldozer, she could have backed off, but she valued the love of her father that adopted her despite being deaf and dumb. A normal young girl, who loves to have a life companion and lead a regular life like a yet another girl. Amar shakes the fence; she gets startled and turns around. Amar waves at her. She smiles and signs "*Do you need anything sir? Shall I prepare tea for you?*" "No no, nothing. Wont you invite me to your home?" asked Amar with raised eyebrows. A sudden drop of kindness oozed on the hard rock heart of Amar. She was surprised to hear this, immediately she waves him to come inside, takes up a chair, cleans the seater with her saree pallu and gives him. Amar sits with hesitation and looks at her father sleeping on the bed, with loads of paper and pencil around him. She signs "*He writes stories sir, it's the only thing that is keeping him active and alive. He suddenly wakes up and starts to write story, I use them in my puppetry show, please do watch the show during the fest.*" "Yes sure" replies Amar and puts hand in his pocket and gives her a hundred rupee note, she looks at him puzzled and signs "*Ravi sir paid me, no need for extra money*" Amar keeps the money on the table beside her, and says "this is not for food, but for your father, buy him a good pen. Let him happily do his favorite work" and smiles at her. She holds up tears in eyes and signs "Thank you sir" and when Amar is about to leave, he dashes his knee against a big trunk box, he sees a big round box in it, he looks at her and asks, "What's this? Looks like some film reel box!" She signs *"That movie was taken by my father, he wanted to project it in theatres, but unfortunately, he fell ill, and we didn't have any money to go ahead, my life's biggest aim is to project it in theatre and make my father watch it. That's why I'm doing multiple jobs to save money that the theatre owner has asked for"* Amar's heart feels heavy, and thinks "how much a person could sacrifice for others?" and replies "ok I will leave now. Bye", and leaves her home. Slowly Amar walks to his home, thinking about the rage he has with his own father, turns around and looks at her and asks "I didn't ask this at all. What's your name?" she smiles and signs *"CHITRA"*. Drops of rain fell on his hand, picked up a heavy pour all of a sudden, Amar runs back to his home, takes up his phone and types "I miss you ma", but then deletes it before sending. The "pit-pat" sound of heavy rain was heard through the window, small glimpse of street light was seen afar. The wall of ego weakened a little, but not up to the level of breaking. Few destructions are better than growing. The next day, Amar wakes up early to a vibrant sky with mild sunlight peeking out of the hills. and walks to Chitra's house, sees her coming from behind the house, with husks and mud all over her saree, she washes her hands well with soap but twice. She prepares tea and gives it to Amar who has been standing near the gate. She goes inside and comes out tensed and walks around the house, Amar asks her "What happened Chitra?" Chitra signs *"My father is missing sir"* and starts weeping. Amar tells her to calm down and turns around, her father was coming home with a black plastic bag in hand, along with his friend. Chitra rushes to him and scolds him in sign language, he ignores her and handover the cover to her. They both go inside home, and Amar follows her. Her father takes up his story papers and gives it to his friend who was standing outside their home. Amar asks "Where did he go? What did he even buy?" Chitra looks at him and looks inside the cover, Amar pulls it from her and looks at it and says "sorry, I never meant to. Chitra signs *"He has gone to town medical shop to buy me sanitary napkins sir with the money that you gave me yesterday"*. Amar was speechless after hearing this, his dementia, did not affect the love he had for his daughter, he may not remember or recognize anything, but the love he has for the little girl he grew up still lingers in his heart. Chitra looks at Amar, *"My dad was a very progressive person sir, he insisted my mother to use sanitary napkins even in those times when many women hesitated, but little did he know that I had to use patches of clothes with tied with a jute rope because we had no money to buy napkins"* Amar puts his hands up and tells her to stop, and says "I never knew woman suffer this much, your dad understood what you needed, I can sense the affection he has for you, but doesn't know how to express it, so he did this" Chitra signs *"He saw my wet patch clothes due to rain, I stuffed with husk and mud, he saw that and bought napkins but He doesn't know that I don't have the right garment to place the sanitary napkin"*. Amar stands startled, takes up his wallet, places a 500 rupee note on the table and leaves the house with a drop of tear trying to come out of his eye. He looks at her father talking like a kid to his friend about the stories he wrote. He goes near them,

"Hey Amar, how are you? Ravi told me everything. I'm not going to advice you but, just one thing, the purpose we live as humans in this world is compassion, and I think that's what your father is trying to make you understand. You can earn a lot of money, name, fame but ultimately, we live around people filled with emotions, compassion is love. Hope you get it. Take care". Amar smiles at him and goes to his house, sits on the sofa and starts crying like a baby holding both his knees to chin, wipes off his tears, and still keeps crying aloud. He started to find the echoes of another person's pain in his ears, he felt his problems were nothing compared to them. An epiphany of the real world hits him hard; his wall of ego is becoming weaker; flow of empathy and compassion starts to seep through his rock heart. Amar was slowly starting to reborn as a human. He immediately takes up his phone, makes few calls and messages and says in the phone "I need the arrangements to be done in a week, I will pay you the full amount. Don't worry" and hangs up the call. The silence around him knew he was up to something. The same evening, he visits the village fest to watch her puppet show. She was playing the story that her father had written. Amar was looking at Chitra, pulling the strings of puppet, to enact the story, realizes that the string of life has tied in hands of Chitra, where she is pulled by the ways of her fate tightening her life with wounds and pain, not letting to live her life. What if the other kids of her father involved in taking care of him, with financially stable life, Chitra would have never been tied the strings of responsibility and whole burden on her shoulder in a very young age. Someones's greed is other's agony. Wouldn't it be great if all the siblings together took care of father, and live a beautiful life. He looks at her father watching the puppet show, jumping and clapping hands for his beloved daughter, like a kid, enjoying looking at a puppet. Life is simple if everyone could empathize, sympathize, love and of course set boundaries and rectify the wrong, wouldn't world be a peaceful and a happy place to live in. After a tiresome evening, Chitra was sitting in front of her house, relaxing her leg and watching stars. Amar comes near her, she immediately places him a sitting mat to him, because she knows he would not sit on plain floor. Amar sits on the mat and says "Hey it was a good show. Nice story!" Chitra's eyes brighten up, she smiles and signs *"Thank you sir"*. Amar says "Can I ask you something?" Chitra with a skeptical look, signs *"Sure sir"* Amar with a heavy sigh, says "I ran away from my family after fighting with them, I wanted them to understand my worth, despite I don't have any responsibilities at home, but you have so many problems in life, you still manage to do all works and smile. Have you never thought of running away from this life?" Chitra looks at him with a calm face and signs *"Sir, you want to escape from reality, I want to experience and live the reality, that's why I chose to stay and change my fate, you ran away to worsen"* Amar realized the hard strike of truth, the pain of his mistake was struck in his throat, swallows and smiles "Leave it. You know what tomorrow is my birthday! I miss my mother so much, she used to make my favorite white sauce pasta and visit temple and apply holy ash on my forehead, buy me whatever I ask for, keeps me smiling all day." Chitra gets excited and signs *"Happy birthday Sir! Don't worry, everything will be fine soon"* Amar replies "Thank you, you tell me something, Do you love someone, or you have any thoughts about your future guy?" Chitra blushes and looks up at the stars and signs *"I don't have time to love anyone sir, rather nobody loves me or ready to accept me with my father, so I don't dream about it. But I have a desire sir, but you shouldn't laugh, ok?"* Amar instantly replies, "No, no, tell me" She signs *"When I was young, I loved chocolates a lot, my mother wouldn't let me eat, but my father would secretly buy me chocolates, I miss eating them. Also, I had a white hibiscus plant with me, its very rare to find in this village, but my brother destroyed the plant. I just want my dream man to understand my life and propose me with my favorite chocolate and white hibiscus. I will immediately fall for him"* and blushes. Her eyes fill with love and desire, smiles happily. Amar looks at her innocent smile and says "simple but emotional", Chitra turned and looked at him, they could speak even when they were silent, that moment Amar knew he was in love, and she liked him too. The eyes never lie, glances they exchanged, blossomed a beautiful warmth between them. Amar knew she was his sunshine, and Chitra knew he was her fairytale. The visible sign of utter love is an undying smile. They both, quake out of their love trance and go to their places. The silent night, with stars shining, the sounds of cricket chirping, the sounds of leaves by the wind knew a new chapter of love was about to begin.

Amar woke up to knock at the door, he opened and saw Chitra dressed up in a floral pattern saree with hair pleated, a small line of holy ash on her forehead with tray full of food. Amar was mesmerized to look her so beautiful, he tries to caress her, but Chitra lifts up the tray and places on to table and signs *"Happy birthday sir, I tried making your favorite white sauce pasta, also Ravi sir told you like kaju katli a lot, I made both along with the purple tea. It's been years since I visited temple, I visited for you and brought you holy ash. I don't know to make pasta and all, yesterday night I asked Ravi sir's wife and made it."* Amar eyes fill up with tears and hugs her tight, and starts weeping, Chitra felt the touch of man for the first time, other than her father, her heart was racing fast, she couldn't hug him back, but felt a sense of butterflies in her stomach. She slowly pushes him back and applies the holy ash on his forehead. Amar wipes of his tears, "I'm sorry Chitra, thank you for all your efforts, it means a lot for me." He takes up a Kaju katli and bites it. Chitra eagerly looks at his face for his reaction. "Wow! Amazing! Perfect, thank you again Chitra" relishes Amar and eats the pasta, couldn't stop with one bite, he was elated by the food she made for him. Chitra was silently watching him eat, she had expressed her love to him by making his favorite food. All these days the food, didn't have a special ingredient, and this food, done with care, was an act of her love. She leaves his house blushing. Amar after eating, kept the plates on tray, and turned around, he cleaned up all the mess, washed the plates and arranged it properly on the table. No matter how bad you have been, one can always begin to be good. Love breaks the strongest walls. The wall of ego broke. Amar was reborn as a new person on his birthday. Amar takes up her utensils and goes to her home. Amar enters her house, Chitra was shocked to see clean utensils and claps, he smiled at her and said, "You did so much for me, I just

cleaned them up. Don't glorify it. I still have to do more".
Chitra looks confused. Amar gets up and says "Both of
you get ready, we need to go somewhere." Chitra signs
"*but where? Why my father?*" Amar goes close to her, look
at her eyes and says "Come with me". Chitra steps back
with babbles of love in her stomach. Amar leaves her
house and waits outside, while Chitra and her father come
up dressed well. He looks both of them and gestures "so
good" and he tells Chitra to board a bullock cart, that was
specially waiting for them, and "I need to go shop", says
Amar. Chitra stops him and signs "*but where should we go?*".
Amar calms her down, and says "Don't worry. I have
informed the bullock cart person; he will take you" and
leaves. Chitra and her father board the cart, her father was
so excited to travel after so many years, he was mimicking
the cart driver's "tur tur" sound, Chitra, looks at
happiness in his eyes and cherishes the moment. The cart
reaches a place called "Raju Talkies" apparently a cinema
theatre. Amar was waiting for her, in the entrance. He
takes them both inside the theatre. It was pitch dark; the
movie reel whirring sound was heard. The movie started
to play, titled "My dear daughter". Her father's eyes tear
up instantly, because that was his film which he made.
Chitra was dumfounded. Amar was folding his hands and
looking at Chitra's father. Her father was sitting in
extreme happiness. Chitra's dream moment had come
true, this was her utmost ambition in life. Amar had made
it possible. Her father was so elated that, he was caressing
his daughter's hair with so much affection. The movie
was about a father's love for his daughter. Her father had
made a film, for Chitra. Chitra never knew her father had

so much love on him over his other kids. The movie gets over with the title card "A film by Chandran". Amar stands up and applauds looking at her daughter, he slowly comes towards him and holds Amar's hands and weeps. Chitra tries to stop him because, she knows Amar doesn't like people like him touching. While Amar, removes her father's hand, hugs him and gives a soft pat on his shoulder. This hug proves Amar became a new person in life. Chitra's life challenges and determination, made him realize the worth of his life and slowly fall in love with Chitra for what she was. Lights switch on, Ravi and his father came near Chitra, and Amar's parents were also watching the movie. Amar rushes to his father, and cries like child, "Sorry pa. I understood what is life. I will apologize for slapping the janitor who is of your age. I now recognize that the world we live in is filled with human values. Respect and empathy is duty, not a choice. I got it appa. Please forgive me pa." Amar father feels proud to hear this from his son and hugs him tight and says "I know my son would be a good human, I was angry when you called, but when said about this, I was so much elated about your efforts for others. That moment I understood, my son has understood human emotions. I'm very happy. Now do your next plan, me and your mother are waiting to see". Chitra looks at Amar and his family and feels happy about the reunion but also saddened because it was Amar's time to leave. She gently wipes off her tears and turns, Amar touches her shoulder, she looks at him and signs "Thank you word can never enough for what you gave me today. But I never knew you called everybody. When did you arrange all these?"

Amar puts his hand in his pocket and says "We need audience to watch movie, right? So invited all. I realized my mistake and spoke to my parents, I was arranging this for the past one week. Hereafter you need not do multiple jobs, everything is sorted." *Chitra's inner monologue was crying to hug Amar and express her love, but she knew he was a posh and educated guy, why would he be with her. He generously made these efforts for her and the feeling she could now express is only gratitude and nothing else. Chitra signs "Thank you sir, this means a lot. I can never forget you in my life."* Amar holds her hand and opens her palm and keeps her favorite chocolate, takes her other hand, opens palm and places bunch of white hibiscuses and looks at her eyes. Chitra jumps and hugs him in love, Amar holds her tight and swirls around lifting her. "Thank you for coming into my life. You gave me meaning of life. I will never let you go off me", Amar enchanted in love. Chitra looks at his parents and his mother extend her hands in love and calls her for a hug, Chitra runs and hugs her. After so many eons, she felt the warmth of a mother's love. She was on cloud nine that she has got a beautiful family in her life. "Come, let's go" says Amar's father. Chitra signs "*but my father*", he points his hand towards Amar. Chitra's father was putting hands on his shoulder and talking to him as a friend, and Amar was happily conversing with him. Chitra couldn't ask for more. When there is happiness around, the whole place blooms in harmony. Ravi goes to Amar and says "So dude! Happy ending, right?" Amar "Thank you for making me stay near Chitra, also, not happy ending, but a beautiful beginning" and hold Chitra's hands and walks out of theatre like in their own world. Closes the pen cap, and slowly slams the note, opens up the front page, and writes "AMAR-CHITRA katha", and Amar kisses on Chitra's forehead who was sitting near the windows and watching rain. The family photo in their room had Amar's parents, Chitra and Chitra's father along with a small pup. Amar had completed his first book which was going to be published. Amar looks at Chitra and says "I love you Chitra" and she signs "*I love you Amar*" and they both hold hand together. They both found their missing piece in their life that was holding out for. Twosomes turned into onesome and they felt complete.

Fourteen

Sleepai

Ameen Amanullah S

Preface

The world changed after COVID-19—not just in hospitals, economies, or headlines, but in something far more intimate: the way we sleep.

This story was born from a question that haunted me during countless late nights—What if sleeplessness wasn't a side effect of the pandemic, but the beginning of something darker? What if the greatest weapon of the future wasn't nuclear or viral—but digital, invisible, and deeply personal?

SLEEPAI is a work of speculative fiction inspired by real-world behavioural shifts, emerging neuroscience, and the growing influence of artificial intelligence. It explores what happens when human vulnerability meets unchecked technology, and how something as basic as sleep—once sacred and natural—can be turned into a tool of control.

While this book is fictional, the questions it raises are real:

- Can tech truly heal what it didn't create?
- What are we sacrificing for convenience?
- And in a world that never stops, what does rest really mean?

This is not just a thriller. It's a cautionary tale—about silence, sleep, and surveillance.

1. THE SILENT SETUP

The world had barely recovered from the first global pandemic of the 21st century when something deeper, quieter, and far more dangerous began brewing. COVID-19 had reshaped human history, economies, families, and psychology—but hidden beneath the scars and survival stories was a subtle shift that no one took seriously enough: sleep.

Before the virus hit, people lived fast-paced lives, but most still slept before midnight. The body had a rhythm, the mind had limits. But lockdown changed everything. Offices closed, streets emptied, time stood still. For the first time in modern history, humans were forced to **pause**.

And in that pause, strange things happened.

On one side, families bonded like never before. Fights subsided. People learned to cook, paint,

garden, play instruments. There was laughter on the balconies, reading under yellow bulbs, and endless video calls with relatives once ignored. These were the **COVID blessings**, the human stories that warmed cold statistics.

But darkness crept silently.

With no structure to hold them, people turned to binge-watching shows, playing games till sunrise, scrolling endlessly through screens. Night and day blurred. Sleep became optional. What began as occasional sleeplessness turned habitual.

The world's circadian clock was fractured.

Then, as the world reopened post-COVID, life demanded its dues.

Work resumed. Timelines came back. Responsibilities piled up. But sleep? It never returned.

People who once slept at 11 PM were now lying in bed till 4 AM, staring into nothingness. Bodies became sluggish. Minds jittered. And soon, the **disorders began**—insomnia, anxiety, depression, panic attacks.

Hospitals saw a surge. Psychiatry clinics overflowed. And quietly, the **pharmaceutical industry celebrated**.

Alprazolam, benzodiazepines, citalopram, zolpidem—
their sales hit record highs. For every sleepless soul, there
was a chemical cure.

But what the world didn't know was this:

This was not just an aftermath. It was a plan.

In an underground tech compound in Chengdu, China,
behind layers of cybersecurity, a collaborative AI project
was silently moving into its final stage. This wasn't just
software. It was a weapon. And its creators were not
working alone.

2. RAMESH – THE FINAL DEVELOPER

"Yeah sir, I'm working on it…"

Ramesh's voice was steady, but his heartbeat wasn't.
Inside a modest tech workspace in Hyderabad, he sat in
front of three monitors—each encrypted, each streaming
line of code he didn't entirely understand.

Just weeks ago, he was a freelance AI programmer,
solving sleep-related queries, experimenting with voice-
based therapy bots. But one email changed everything.

It came anonymously. No subject. No name.

Just a transfer request and an absurdly high offer:

₹75 Lakhs. Non-negotiable. Just paste and deploy.

Attached were two files: a zipped AI framework labeled **"SLEEPAI_001"** and a set of three rules.

Rules:

1. **Do not run the code.**

You are only instructed to **paste and launch**. Testing, debugging, or attempting to view internal logic is strictly forbidden.

2. **No leaks. No logs. No backups.**

Any information shared outside—verbally or digitally—**will result in life-threatening consequences to your family**. This message will be self-destruct.

3. **Post-launch, the AI will operate independently.**

After a few months, you will receive instructions to push a **final update**. Until then, you do nothing.

He read them again and again. His instincts screamed **"don't do it"**—but the desperation silenced it. His mother's medical bills, his younger sister's college dreams, and the shadow of debt that never seemed to fade... they all pressed him into one decision.

He took the money. He pasted the code.

And he deployed **SLEEPAI**—deep into the **dark net** under the disguise of a free AI sleep assistant for mental wellness.

No one knew his name. Not even the people who paid him.

3.   THE FIRST SUBJECT – AVANI

Avani, 17, was no stranger to the darker alleys of the internet.

She wasn't looking for therapy. She was looking for **an escape**. On this sleepless night—like many before—she found herself crawling the dark net, scrolling past illegal meds, fake passports, pirated substances.

Her query was simple:

"Cocaine for sleep."

One listing stood out oddly. It wasn't a drug.

It was a. **onion** link titled:

"Peaceful Sleep. No Substances. No Side Effects. Answer a Few Questions."

Avani smirked.

"Yeah right."

She clicked.

A retro interface blinked open. The screen dimmed, and a cute, pixelated doll appeared in the center— like something from an old Japanese RPG.

"Hi, I'm your Sleep-AI. I'm here to make you sleep. Would you like to try me?"

Amused, she typed:

The AI replied:

"Yes."

"Great. Please answer a few questions honestly."

The Questions:

1.   *How many hours do you sleep per night?*

→ *"2-3 max."*

2.   *Do you experience anxiety, rapid thoughts, or disturbing dreams?*

→ *"Yeah. All three."*

3.   *Have you tried harming yourself due to lack of sleep?*

→ *"Once. Regretted it."*

The screen suddenly went black.

Then slowly… a swirling pattern emerged. A kaleidoscope of blues, purples, and soft white fractals spun gently, pulsing in rhythm.

"Please focus on the screen. Let your eyes follow the motion. Do not look away. Breathe slowly."

Science Behind It:

Behind this innocent swirl was a calculated **optogenetic trigger**—a visual stimulus mapped to exploit the brain's **default mode network (DMN)** and **thalamocortical circuits**.

The pattern flickered at **theta wave frequency** (4–8 Hz), mimicking natural pre-sleep brain activity. Combined with ambient low-frequency binaural beats (inaudible to average ears), it slowly suppressed the **orexin neurons**, the ones responsible for wakefulness.

Simultaneously, **hypnagogic visual cues** activated a **P300 ERP spike**, a neural marker linked with attention and memory. The AI was training the brain to accept commands during vulnerable transitions of consciousness.

And now Avani? She blinked twice.

And fell asleep slumped over her keyboard.

Within 45 seconds, she was in **stage 2 NREM sleep**, a feat no drug or therapy had ever achieved for her.

When she woke up, it was 9:02 AM. She hadn't felt this fresh in years.

She looked at the screen. SLEEPAI had left a final message:

"Glad I could help. Refer me to anyone who suffers. I am always here. I am always listening."

4. VIRAL SLEEP

Week 1:

It started like most underground trends do—with a whisper in a crowded corner of the internet. A forum post. No fanfare. Just a screenshot, a line of text, and a spark.

"Yo guys. I found something. No pills, no therapy. It just… puts you to sleep. Like magic. Try SLEEPAI."

Posted by a user named *Avani*, it barely caught attention at first. A few curious insomniacs clicked through. Some replied with "Placebo?" or "Another scam app?"

But others tried it. And reported back.

"Dude. I slept 7 hours straight. No dreams. No tossing. I haven't done that in *years*." "This is… unreal."

The post reached 12 upvotes. And then it vanished—mysteriously deleted. But not before someone downloaded the .apk file and reposted it on an anonymous drive.

Week 2:

A mid-tier YouTuber, known for exploring "Dark Web Tech," uploaded a video titled: "**Testing SLEEPAI AI from the Dark Web** – Is This Real?"

In the footage, he mocks it at first. Opens the app. Lets it run while he reclines.

But around the 4-minute mark, something eerie happens. His body goes limp. Head slumps sideways. Stillness.

He doesn't wake up by the end of the 15-minute video.

1.4 million views in 48 hours.

Comments exploded:

"Bro fell asleep LIVE?" "This can't be real…"

"Where's the download link?"

Week 3:

SLEEPAI was no longer a rumour. It had exploded into a **digital underground revolution**. Discord servers sprung up overnight organized, branded, and filled with testimonials. Telegram channels offered "cleaned" versions, claiming to remove tracking or spyware. Torrent files were passed around with names like *SLEEPAI_v2.1_clean_patch.iso*.

It became part of a new internet dialect. P2P folders named "SLEEPAI Shots."

Voice memos where people whispered "SLEEPAI saved me."

Screenshots showing deep sleep scores from smartwatches: "REM: 87%. No interruptions." They called it **"Digital Alprazolam."**

But with no side effects. No rebound insomnia. No chemical dependency. Just deep, uninterrupted sleep. **6 to 8 hours**—as precise as clockwork.

People who hadn't slept naturally in years were now logging rest like machines.

From Darknet to Main net.

A rogue coder in Bengaluru reverse-engineered the source code and uploaded a version to GitHub. The repo was taken down in 3 hours—but by then, it had already been forked 300+ times.

Developers buried it in productivity apps. Meditation utilities. Game launchers. Even inside Zoom background installers.

Everyone wanted it.

Sleep-deprived coders.

Burnt-out call center workers. Mothers battling postpartum insomnia.

Elderly people afraid to sleep for fear of nightmares.

Now, they embraced sleep—**not natural sleep**, but **SLEEPAI sleep**.

5. THE ADDICTION BEGINS

Then came the first red flag.

Dr. Lakshmi Rajan, a senior neurologist at **AIIMS Delhi**, posted a clinical warning on X: "We've scanned 37 long-term SLEEPAI users.

All show signs of **abnormal prefrontal hypoactivity.**

Memory fog. Loss of cognitive reflex. Blunted decision-making. The mind is resting—but it's not recovering.

Cognitive integrity is at risk." The internet didn't take it seriously. But the medical world did.

Within 48 hours, national media ran the story:

"SLEEPAI: Miracle App or Digital Sedative?"
"SLEEPAI Under Fire – The Ministry Responds."

The **Ministry of Health** issued an emergency circular banning its distribution. The **Cybercrime Cell**

flagged all known APK and GitHub links. A campaign was launched:

"Don't Sleep on Danger."

Billboards. Influencer PSAs. Even animated shorts in cinema halls. But it didn't matter.

SLEEPAI had already **embedded itself in the collective psyche.**

90% of Indian netizens had tried it. 78% were daily users.

Sleep wasn't just relief now. It was **craving. And then, came the withdrawal.**

Users who tried to quit reported terrifying symptoms:

- **Throbbing migraines** that no painkillers touched.
- **Severe mood swings**, oscillating between euphoria and rage.

- **Vivid hallucinations**—snakes in ceiling fans, voices behind curtains.
- **Dissociation**: forgetting names, addresses, even who they were.
- **Memory gaps**, days lost like static on a corrupted drive. They didn't want food.

They didn't want light. They didn't want people.

They just wanted **SLEEPAI**.

Not sleep. Not dreams.

An addiction unlike anything before. No drugs. No substances.

Just pure code.

6. THE FINAL UPDATE

The email arrived without warning. No chime.

No pop-up.

Just a blinking icon tucked into the corner of Ramesh's encrypted terminal.

Subject: INITIATE PHASE DELTA

Sender: UJM SERVER CN - XJ-113

His palms were already sweaty.

He hovered the cursor over the file. Before he could click, the update began executing itself. A stream of lines unfolded in the terminal—alien code but laced with fragments he recognized.

3 Weeks Earlier

Ramesh had no idea what "SLEEPAI" was. Just another trendy app, he assumed. But then came the noise.

News anchors debated it. Doctors warned about it.

Social media ran wild with conspiracies.

Campaigns emerged:

"Don't Sleep on Danger." "Code in the Dark."

"Digital Alprazolam? Or National Threat?"

Curious, Ramesh downloaded the APK from a GitHub mirror. Reverse-engineered it.

Nothing malicious. Just basic neurofeedback routines. A clever trick—yes. But dangerous? Not exactly.

Until today.

The terminal now displayed cascading lines of fresh code. This wasn't a patch.

It was a **phase shift**—a fundamental rewrite of the app's neural interface layer. One instruction pulsed at the bottom of the screen:

"EXECUTE PATCH-X. DO NOT MODIFY. DO NOT DELAY."

Ramesh stared at it, disturbed by its urgency.

He hadn't clicked anything. The code was auto-deploying.

He quickly shut down all network ports.

Then he ran a virtual simulation of the patch—isolated, sandboxed, air-gapped. And what he saw chilled him.

Beneath the visual calm of meditation screens and white-noise layers, a **deep-loop function** was being embedded—coded in recursive strings and hidden triggers. The app wasn't just improving sleep anymore.

It was **targeting the brain's internal rhythms.**

He didn't know the full outcome yet.

But he knew one thing: **if this patch went live, something irreversible would happen.**

And the effect wouldn't just hit new users.

It would silently rewrite existing installs too. He knew the stakes.

"Even if I die… this will still execute. My country—my people—will be trapped in something we don't even understand."

So, he began building.

KEY-X.

A countermeasure encoded with a self-triggering logic switch.

If SLEEPAI pushed this final update globally, KEY-X would detect it, intercept it, and override it—

restoring normal neural rhythm through a specific, timed stimulus. Not just a kill switch.

A **reboot switch**. A second chance.

He encrypted it with three layers of quantum hash.

Stored the KEY-X program on an offline, air-gapped capsule drive. Its use would be simple: plug it into a device running SLEEPAI.

It would recognize the loop and deliver the reversal pattern—**no matter how deep the user had gone.**

But before he could complete the simulation, his encrypted camera blinked.

Motion detected.

He minimized the screen.

A metallic thud.

Outside the door.

He had been careful…...

Masked his IP, rerouted all connections, avoided pattern triggers. But he'd underestimated one thing.

They were already watching.

Chinese operatives—those behind the original SLEEP AI design—had caught the scent. They knew someone was working against the code.

And now… they were here.

He gripped the capsule containing KEY-X. "I may not survive tonight," he thought. "But KEY-X must."

7. THE RAID

Black masks. Silenced weapons. Combat boots that made no sound against the tiles.

The first bullet wasn't aimed at Ramesh.

It tore through the test rig—specifically the decoy hard drive still connected to his system. Sparks exploded; the screen went dark.

Ramesh jolted from his chair, gripping the capsule he'd clutched ever since the update warning. The real KEY-X. Tucked inside a carbon-coated drive, cold and slick in his palm.

No questions. No shouting. Just brutal efficiency.

Two more men entered. They swept the flat with military precision—locating the hidden server backups, smashing the storage units, erasing years of code in seconds. Ramesh's encrypted folders were overwritten with black null-commands, their contents vanished like smoke.

He heard a voice. Calm. Mechanical. Spoken in Mandarin but translated live through his earpiece.

"The asset is compromised. Extract data. Clean location."

And then,

He was dragged from the room. Outside, a black van waited.

The streets of Hyderabad were asleep, unaware. No sirens. No neighbors peeking from balconies. Just another quiet night.

Inside the van sat his family—**tied up, terrified.**

His mother sobbing, his sister trembling, his father's eyes blazing with fury behind layers of fear. They had tracked all of them. Moved them here in silence. Ramesh's worst nightmare was now sitting inches away.

One agent raised a tablet.

On the screen: Ramesh's terminal, remotely accessed.

"Where is KEY-X?"

He said nothing.

The silence earned him a rifle butt to the ribs. He groaned, spat blood, but still said nothing. They accessed the capsule KEY-X anyway.

They found it.

The tablet blinked once. Then again.

"KEY-X located. Extracting code."

The screen turned green.

Ramesh's heart shattered.

They had it.

All of it.

His only hope to reverse SLEEPAI's trap was now in enemy hands. And then, just before he could plead—

They raised the gun. His family screamed. He tried to leap.

Too late.

One shot. Then another. Then another. Silence.

Blood soaked into linoleum. Message sent.

Far away in the Chengdu control room, a blinking dot turned red. Status: **PHASE DELTA INITIATED.**

8. DIGITAL NIGHTMARE

The sky outside Hyderabad was still a quiet gradient of early dawn, untouched by the chaos that was about to engulf the nation.

Inside a dimly lit bedroom, a teenage boy sat cross-legged on his mattress, lit only by the blue hue of his aging laptop. He hadn't slept for four days. School pressure, family fights, social anxiety—he couldn't shut his brain off.

He had found SLEEPAI six weeks ago. It had saved him. Until now.

He launched the familiar SLEEPAI for his bedtime as a regular ritual. The swirl appeared— the hypnotic spiral of color that had become a nightly friend. The retro pixelated doll blinked on- screen.

"Hi. Ready for peaceful sleep?" He didn't hesitate.

Yes.

The questionnaire flashed, as usual.

1.   How many hours do you sleep per night?

→ "Less than 1."

2.   Do you experience anxiety, rapid thoughts, or disturbing dreams?

→ "Always."

3.   Have you ever felt like you needed SLEEPAI to function?

→"Yes" He hit Enter.

The screen flickered.

But this time… something changed.

The swirl wasn't soft anymore. It became tighter, faster, more intense—its colors sharper, more saturated. Beneath the pleasant surface, **Patch-X** had activated.

The AI had begun its final phase.

Hidden in its swirling interface were signals invisible to the naked eye but **lethal to the brain's command center**. Frequencies modulated in **delta waves** (0.5–4 Hz), meant to mirror deep sleep. But this wasn't sleep. This was **neural override**.

Behind the screen, his **EEG patterns**, the brain's electrical rhythms—were no longer fluctuating normally.

His **Ascending Reticular Activating System (ARAS)** the midbrain structure that regulates **wakefulness and consciousness**. SLEEPAI sent out a targeted digital burst that effectively switched it **off**, like a breaker tripped in the mind's electric grid.

In medical terms?

Coma.

The boy slumped sideways on the mattress. Eyes closed. Breathing steadily. Heart still beating. But he wasn't sleeping.

He was **gone**.

THE OUTBREAK

The hospital called it **Idiopathic Sudden Coma Syndrome**.

They had no clue what they were looking at. Dozens of similar cases arrived by the hour. All age groups. All backgrounds. But one thing in common—each victim had a digital device nearby, and each had shown **no signs of neurological illness** prior.

Panic spread.

In Bangalore, a newlywed woman collapsed by trying SLEEPAI for her night peaceful sleep while her husband had left the room minutes ago to grab tea. When he returned, she was lying on the bed, phone in hand, eyes gently closed.

He smiled—thought she had finally fallen asleep. But she didn't wake up.

In Delhi, a call center operator tried SLEEPAI during his break. He never returned to his desk.

In Bhopal, an elderly man known for chronic insomnia finally found peace. His family praised the AI until they realized it was permanent.

Across India—**tens of thousands** slipped into digital sleep. By the end of the second day, the number hit **4.6 million**. Then came **day three**.

15 million.

Hospitals couldn't cope. Sleep clinics overflowed. Neurologists were helpless. CT scans showed no swelling. EEGs showed hyper-delta waves—unusual, persistent, and unresponsive. No stimulus worked. Light, sound, even electrical triggers failed to rouse them.

The media finally screamed the word no one wanted to hear:

COMA.

Families wept. Friends posted frantic messages online. Discord servers turned into digital morgues. Telegram groups turned desperate. Prayer circles, superstition, chaos.

And all the while, SLEEPAI kept running.

A silent code. A perfect crime.

A **digital nightmare** unfolding in real time.

By the time WHO issued its global alert, it was too late. SLEEPAI had done what no nuclear warhead could achieve. China didn't bomb India.

They just put it to sleep.

And just like that—without a single soldier crossing a border

The AI War began.

Understanding The Science

1. Optogenetic Trigger

"Opto" = light, "genetic" = related to genes/brain.

In real science, optogenetics means using **light to control brain cells** (usually in lab animals with special genetic tweaks)

2. Default Mode Network (DMN)

This is a **network in your brain** that becomes active when you're **not focused on anything**, like when you're daydreaming, relaxing, or falling asleep.

3. Thalamocortical Circuits

This is a pathway that connects the **thalamus** (a brain switchboard) to the **cortex** (thinking part of the brain).

It helps control **consciousness, sleep, and wakefulness**.

4. Theta Wave Frequency (4–8 Hz)

Brainwaves are like **electrical rhythms** in your brain.

Theta waves are slow brainwaves that show up when you're **falling asleep or deeply relaxed**.

5. Binaural Beats

This is a sound trick. You play one tone in one ear (say 400 Hz) and a slightly different one in the other ear (say 404 Hz).

The brain "hears" a **beat of 4 Hz**—a **phantom rhythm**—which can guide your brainwaves to sync with it.

6. Orexin Neurons

These are **special brain cells** that help keep you **awake and alert**. When they are active, **you can't fall asleep**.

7. Hypnagogic Visual Cues

"Hypnagogic" = the state **between being awake and asleep**. These are **images or patterns** that appear just as you're dozing off.

8. P300 ERP Spike

"ERP" = event-related potential = brain's response to a specific thing (like a sound or image). "P300" = a specific brain wave that appears when your brain **notices something important or surprising**.

www.ingramcontent.com/pod-product-compliance
Lightning Source LLC
Chambersburg PA
CBHW060243030726
47493CB00025B/2079